Drawing Amanda

Stephanie Feuer

DENVER, COLORADO

For permission requests, quantity sales or special discounts,
please write to the publisher below.

HIPSOMEDIA
8151 East 29th Avenue
Denver, Colorado 80238
info@hipsomedia.com
www.hipsomedia.com

Publisher's Note: This is a work of fiction. Names, characters,
places, and incidents are a product of the author's imagination.
Locales and public names are sometimes used for atmospheric
purposes. Any resemblance to actual people, living or dead, or
to businesses, companies, events, institutions, or locales is
completely coincidental.

Drawing Amanda / Stephanie Feuer – 1st ed.
ISBN-13: 9780988739444 • ISBN-10: 0988739445
Juvenile Fiction / Computers
Juvenile Fiction / Social Issues / Strangers

Illustrations by S.Y. Lee

This book is dedicated to you, yes you, the reader, who could be doing other things but chose to read right now. Good choice. And thank you.

HIPSO BOOK CLUB

To learn about new titles, new authors, special discounts and what's hip at Hipso Media, please sign-up for our free Hipso Book Club at join@hipsomedia.com.

Drawing Amanda

I N THE HISTORY OF SCHOOL LUNCHES, no one had ever paid this much attention to a side salad. Inky Kahn swatted a straggle of his long hair away from his face, scrunched up his storm gray eyes and tried to conjure the exact green of the iceberg lettuce in Amanda's bowl.

He wanted his drawing of her to be perfect, and focusing on the right shade helped. He knew he was rusty; last year he'd filled his notebooks with abstracts, a mad rush of color, emotion running like muck. Rivers of guilt traversing the page.

There were definitely peas in her salad. He remembered how Amanda balanced one on her fork while she laughed (she laughed!) at his story about how he got his nickname. And asparagus? Did she have asparagus? Are there even asparagus in October?

The top of his chest throbbed as if his heart had been pushed up, displaced by grief, his insides swollen from the burden he carried. He bit his lip as he struggled to recall the items on her lunch tray, then stroked a single line of black ink on the page before him. There were things that actually mattered in the world, Inky knew, and just in case he'd forgotten, his school, Manhattan's prestigious Metropolitan Diplomatic Academy, served up heaps of world tragedy and disaster as part of the curriculum. But at this moment, the world, his world, depended on him drawing Amanda.

Chapter 1
What's New Is Old Again

THE CAFETERIA WAS LOUD. The welcome sign proclaimed in sapphire blue letters that 82 different mother tongues were spoken by Metropolitan Diplomatic Academy students. To Inky, it sounded like they were all being spoken at once. Twelve grades of excitement, none of it his.

The first year in high school, Upper One, didn't promise to be any different from middle school, if the cafeteria was any indication—same blue paint, big gray tables and uncomfortable popsicle-orange plastic chairs. Everyone was sitting at their usual tables, too—everyone who came back.

Inky tucked his head as he passed Curry Hill, where a gaggle of Indian girls shared the right side of the cafeteria with the Math-letes who'd appropriated the table where he used to sit when his old crew was around. They were all now attending the High School of Art & Design. He'd missed too much school last year to bother applying, even though he was the most talented of the group.

He felt a tap on his shoulder. "WB, dude. Welcome back," his friend Rungs said. He was tall and twig-skinny. Over the summer he'd let his black hair go spiky, so he looked like a manga comic character.

Rungs raised his paper cup of coffee and took a big sip. "Jetlag. Got back from Thailand Sunday. Three weeks of mom's cooking." Rungs patted his belly. "And quality time with Apsara, who, IMHO, is prettier than ever. But that's just my humble opinion."

"Excuse me, and WTF," Inky said. "What's with the abbreviations?"

Rungs shrugged.

"You talk like that? You can't talk like that."

Rungs shrugged again. "Souvenir of my nerd summer."

Rungs, short for his last name, Rungsiyaphoratana, was a second generation computer geek. His father did intelligence work for the Thai government, lasting through a string of prime ministers.

There was a momentary commotion as the Frenchies, kids from French-speaking countries or international schools, pushed two tables together, spanning from Curry Hill to the middle of the cafeteria where Sven Thorsson and the Soccer Boys had taken their alpha place in the center.

Inky and Rungs walked toward the back of the cafeteria. "Anything else I should know?" Inky said.

Rungs whipped out a mini pocket computer, sleeker than anything available in U.S. gadget stores. "64 gigs and the pre-release of the super nimbus processor."

The most ethnically-mixed group was a group of girls who sat down in unison like a rehearsal for a Junior Miss World pageant. The Sacred Circle, they called themselves, and they were all stunning in their own way. Hawk stood off to the side, petite but commanding because of her perfect posture and sinewy build. She shook out her dirty blond ponytail and changed from skateboard shoes to ballet flats. She looked up, caught Inky's eye and sneered.

Inky looked away as he and Rungs sat down at the table in the back. "Never heard of it," he said,

"Deep beta."

"Sweet."

"Sweeter." Rungs turned the small, crisp display screen to Inky to show a picture of Apsara, his girl-friend back in Thailand. Inky whistled.

He put his device back in his pocket and said, "Check this out, dude. One of the nerdesses at geek camp told me about a start-up looking for kids to help with a new game. Could be the way to get you some exposure. Catapult you to the working art world. Who needs that art high school?"

Rungs grabbed Inky's pen, the cartridge pen with the swirly green marble design that felt so cool and smooth between his fingers. "Hey," Inky said indignantly.

"Dude, this could be your golden ticket. Recognition. Opportunity. It's a start-up. The launching pad to fortune, my man." Rungs deliberately glanced over at the table where the art students used to sit. "Chill. Don't worry about your pen."

Inky stared at the pen in Rungs's hand. It'd been his father's, and he carried it like a talisman.

"You gotta check this out," Rungs said, ignoring Inky's glare, as he reached for Inky's black sketch notebook.

"Don't touch that," Inky said, covering the pages with his hands.

Rungs rolled his eyes and patted his pockets looking for paper—as if he ever carried any. Then he sighed heavily. Inky couldn't help but smile, but held tight to his sketchpad.

Rungs looked toward the table adjacent to theirs. Inky saw a girl with wild dark hair he didn't recognize sitting alone behind them. Rungs reached his long arm over to her notebook, jiggling the table as he knocked into a chair.

"You don't mind if I borrow a piece of paper?" Rungs said, not waiting for her answer. The girl looked up—her eyes were brown with flecks of gold. Raw umber.

"Hey," she said, stretching out the word. She narrowed her eyes, and the flecks took on a more intense hue. Inky looked at her, then couldn't look away. He knew he was staring. She wasn't classically pretty; her features were a striking mix of pure Anglo and mestizo. It was a pretty he learned to appreciate at MDA—zebra pretty, the girls called it.

Rungs snatched her notebook. She'd reached for it too late. Inky could see the curve of her arm through the stiff white fabric of her shirt.

Rungs opened the notebook to the first page and tapped on the paper to get Inky's attention.

"You can thank me later." Rungs pressed down hard as he wrote down a URL for the test site and a login password.

"Hey, careful. You'll break the nib," Inky said.

Rungs ripped out the piece of paper and handed it to Inky. "GTBOS, my friend. Glad to be of service." Rungs returned the pen to Inky.

He stood up and returned the notebook to the girl, bowing as he put it on the table. She glowered at Rungs, then Inky, and then her notebook. She reminded Inky of Picasso's girl with a ponytail. Her look was muse-worthy; her face had depth, beauty and imperfections. Her gaze made Inky think of light streaming through a window crack.

"Thanks. It'll come back to you," Rungs said to her in a way that sounded like a promise or an omen.

Chapter 2
Inky Signs On

HOMEWORK ON THE FIRST DAY should be against the law, Inky thought, as the books in his backpack bounced against his spine on his walk home. The big tree outside his building cast a long shadow; the few fallen leaves were like an orange arrow pointing home.

Inky climbed the stairs to his apartment. Inside it was dark and had a musty smell that was comfortingly familiar. He tossed the mail on the living room chair, releasing dust particles that danced in the light leaking through the venetian blinds.

In the narrow hallway, Inky's backpack snagged on the black nylon fabric that was stretched over the hall mirror. Behind the fabric he could just make out the pattern of its richly-carved wood frame—a souvenir from his father's trip to Sri Lanka. Inky pictured the cinnamon wood he could not see and headed to the back of the apartment where his room and his father's study overlooked the street.

Inky had to be careful not to bump his head on the loft bed above his desk. An old photograph of himself was taped to a narrow slab of fake stone, a discarded kitchen counter that Inky and his father had found on the street. It sat on two sawhorses and doubled as a drafting table. The space was fine when he was young, but now that he was fourteen, it felt cramped. He threw his books on the faded blue carpeting, even though it would have been easier to use the big desk in his father's study.

The study was just as his father had left it before his last trip; they'd barely dared to disturb the dust.

Although they'd never been very religious, when the rabbi gave them instructions after the funeral, Inky and his mother took the words almost literally. During *shiva*, the Jewish period of mourning, all mirrors in the house are covered and mourners don't get haircuts or wear new or freshly laundered clothes.

Neither Inky nor his mother had felt much like cleaning after the *shiva* period was over. Soon they were moving things only when they absolutely had to, sweeping merely as a distraction from grief. A year and a half later, the house was unkempt by habit, like one of those sorry ladies in sweatpants you see at the supermarket. When Inky passed the deli down the street, sometimes he'd smell the bleach they tossed on the sidewalk. It smelled sweet to him. His father had been the tidy one.

Shiva, the Hebrew word for seven, lasts for a week, the rabbi had told them. Then the candle is blown out, the mirrors uncovered, the shades raised. The mourners take a walk around the block, a symbolic step back into the world, into the light.

But Inky's house was still dark.

He parted the curtain to the lair underneath his bed and bent his head. Unlike last year when he couldn't and didn't concentrate on his work, this year he'd sworn he'd try. He wished he was in the same core class as Rungs, but at least he was not with Sven and Demos from the soccer team.

Inky logged on to his computer to see his social studies assignment. He skimmed the type-dense paragraphs his teacher had posted about the importance of social anthropology. The teacher, trying to be hip, suggested they look at their Facebook pages to see the structure of their "tribes." So much for fresh starts. He'd abandoned his page last year.

At least he knew he wanted to be an artist, and maybe he didn't need a specialized art school to get there. He pulled out the paper Rungs had given him in the cafeteria that morning and typed in the URL and password.

"Welcome to Megaland" resolved across the top of his screen. He liked the chubby type and neon colors. A second later a text line appeared under the neon logo: "Megaland: Become your Dream."

Sure hope so, he thought. A box appeared at the bottom of the screen. "Click to get started."

Inky filled out the sign-in screen. He even created a username, "Picasso2B," the name he used for most sites he visited. A chat box opened on the side.

Megaland: Hello, Picasso2B. Glad to meet you. Megaland will be a game unlike any other, and we're recruiting a core group of special, talented kids to help get it off the ground. Depending on your interests, you can help build scenarios or design beta game modules. Does that sound good to you?

It sure sounded better than doing homework.

Picasso2B: yes

Megaland: Excellent. So let's find out how you'll fit in. A placement survey will pop up on your screen asking you about yourself. Here's me: I was super successful in the music biz. Had a stretch of downtime and got into programming. Now I'm gonna use those skills to create a new breed of game. And you might be one of the ones to help. On the form, tell me what games you're into, your interests and hobbies, the usual stuff.

Inky clicked through the questions. For interests, he typed "design." The questions about games were interactive.

Megaland: Name a favorite game

Picasso2B: video phone or computer?

Megaland: Computer.

Picasso2B: last yr I got back into Spore

Megaland: What drew you to the game?

That was easy—the logline on the box: "Tired of your planet? Build a new one."

Picasso2B: IDK, the advertising I guess

Megaland: What kept you coming back?

Inky loved designing those multi-eyed, gaudy-colored creatures. Their internecine battles had helped to keep the bright hot colors of loss out of his head, at least for a little while.

Picasso2B: The Creature Creator is way cool, especially the animation. Plus it keeps my mind off stuff.

There were more questions—a little annoying, but Rungs said this was a start-up, so it made sense that a cutting-edge game developer would do his research.

Megaland: Ok. Let's switch gears. Describe yourself. What are your best features or what would someone notice about you?

He couldn't quite say. After a year of the mirrors covered in black cloth, he'd gotten out of the habit of looking or caring. Every so often his mother would come out of her haze of distraction and look his way, as if seeing him for the first time. She'd gasp like she'd seen a ghost, and he knew it was because he resembled his father.

Megaland: Please complete each question.

The cursor blinked, wanting more. So Inky typed in the facts.

Picasso2B: tall, light-skinned

He hit return hoping to move on to the next question, but nothing happened.

Megaland: Please provide a complete description before moving on to the next question.

Harsh, Inky thought. He added something he knew people noticed.

Picasso2B: long brown hair

Megaland: What else?

Picasso2B: gray eyes

Megaland: Slim, chunky, athletic?

Picasso2B: not fat, not thin, Y?

Megaland: So we can create your avatar

The cursor blinked. Inky felt tempted to hit escape and sign off, to abandon this like he abandoned everything last year. He thought of what Rungs had said. Having his artwork used in a game could be his big break. And what better way than to get in at the beginning?

The cursor blinked again. Inky thought of it as an arrow pointing him on a new path.

Picasso2B: Can I make my own?

Chapter 3
Amanda in the Glass Tower

AMANDA'S ROOM WAS LIKE ALL the other rooms of the apartment, cold and rectangular with too much glass. It made her think of the fish tanks she saw everywhere when they'd lived in Laos. There it meant good luck. And here? All the glass meant was that the building was too new to have a past.

One whole wall was dominated by a glass window. Most of her stuff was still in boxes stacked against the stark white wall by the closet. She'd unpacked some of her treasures and put them on top of the bright white dresser. Her mother loved white. So crisp, so clean, she'd say. You'd think she was a nurse, but really she just liked to be the most colorful thing in the room.

On the center of her dresser was her wooden game of Go, with the points of the star filled with multicolored glass marbles. She could see a different world in each one. Next to it was a wooden monkey on a string from the market in Nairobi.

Wind-up toys from her father's trips were grouped on the side. The gorilla made a crunchy sound when she wound it up. It spit little sparks of simulated fire as it marched. She wound a little white mouse with ballet-pink ears and sent it scurrying across the dresser. It made her feel better, but not much, not when her brothers weren't around to play along.

Amanda had been dreading the first day of school and the questions people would ask. "Where are you from? Where have you lived?" She knew where she was born—her mother's native Venezuela, the year after the mudslides. But that was hardly where she was *from*; they'd stayed for less than a year. Besides, when someone asked where you were from, they were really asking where you belonged.

She'd rather not have to say anything at all. Shyness was her response to life as a modern nomad. Her father's work with the World Assistance Agency meant that they'd moved every couple of years. As he rose through the organization, he'd chased disasters in Central America; tsunamis in Thailand, Laos and Indonesia; and revolutions in African countries that had since changed their names. He'd been everywhere saving the world. Amanda and her two older brothers, Derek and Kevin, attended the international schools in those places, shielded from it all—in the world, but not of it. Always there was a big house and "help"—a cook, a maid, a driver and security. Always the same. Always different.

Always new people to meet. Amanda never got any better at it.

She'd never really had to before, because she had always had her brothers. If she belonged anywhere, she belonged with them, belonged to the elaborate fantasy worlds they'd created for themselves. But this year Derek was in college at Tufts and Kevin was at a Swiss boarding school.

That morning all the new students were asked to stand up in the auditorium and tell where they were from. Amanda had tried Derek's line: "I'm a citizen of the world." It used to work for him because he had their mother's easy, confident smile and a way of flipping his straight black hair away from his face that highlighted his good looks. It did not work for Amanda, who lacked the flair of self-confidence, and her crazycurl hair was anything but tame.

She was intimidated by being in a grade with a hundred-plus students. Her last school had fifty kids in all the grades combined. Derek's line fell flat and everyone laughed, and not in a nice way.

The principal, Elsbet Harooni, a middle-aged, fair-haired, pixie-like woman who was smaller than many of the students, said, "You'll find we all are citizens of the world at the Metropolitan Diplomatic Academy." She held the podium with her bony fingers and looked at Amanda. The auditorium was uncomfortably silent. Thinking back, Amanda realized the principal must have been waiting for her to say something. But she did not. "Well, Amanda Valdez Bates, we hope you'll call this home."

Ha. This was the coldest place she'd been to yet, and she'd been to Iceland in the winter. The principal's remark made her miss her brothers more than ever. They would have nixed her mother's choice for what to wear on the first day of school to a school where uniforms were not required. Her outfit was all wrong. Only the attendance lady in the main office was dressed in the same magazine chic as Amanda, in a short black skirt and designer white blouse.

"Sacred Circle in the house," a group of girls had said in "core" class, which seemed to replace homeroom at this school. The Sacred Circle girls were dressed in black leggings cut off at the ankles, topped with long, bright or floral oversized shirts, and wore grungy white sneakers covered with magic-markered names and drawings.

"And what do we have here? Hello," said Ellen Monahan, the prototypically-American girl who sat in the row next to Amanda, in a super nasty voice.

One of the other girls touched Amanda's shirt. "Hello dorky white shirt. This is Upper School. Um, we're fourteen now," the girl said too loudly.

They sure didn't talk like that at the Nairobi International School.

Not that coming home was any better. Her mother was giving instructions to the new housekeeper. She was polite, but Amanda heard an edge in her voice, which usually meant her father was having dinner guests.

"Amanda dear, how was school? They loved the skirt, yes? My sophisticated little lady."

Amanda's mother shook her perfectly curled black hair, and hurried Amanda down the hall, her spiky heels clicking on the bare floor. "Shower and dress for dinner, before your homework. You have homework, yes? Your father invited some Foundation people over. Big donors to the water initiative, someone behind a new hospital in Haiti, and, and it's exciting to be in New York, no?"

Amanda stifled the urge to say "really" in that sarcastic way she'd heard in school.

At dinner Amanda watched her father as she would an actor—so funny, so polite, cheerfully holding court. She hardly recognized him as the daddy who would bring home wounded animals and get down in the mud to work with the disaster relief crews he supervised. Now he was the boss of the agency, and the main part of his job was to talk to rich people to get them to pay for all the agency's save-the-world plans. He seemed to enjoy it.

Amanda's father pressed a button and the shades covering the two floor-to-ceiling glass windows of the dining room lowered, making a whirring sound that startled Amanda. As the room darkened, the housekeeper came in with a tray of espresso and pastries. He clicked on a slide show he'd prepared. His greatest hits of disasters, Kevin would have said.

Amanda nabbed a couple of enticing Italian pastries, careful not to block the image of her father and his staff building a hut as part of the tsunami relief effort.

She'd loved Indonesia, going to the beach every day, wearing a swath of batik fabric wrapped over her bathing suit. She hadn't loved Nairobi, especially not the armed guards stationed outside their compound toward the end, and the feeling that no one could be trusted as allegiances changed around them. She felt the tears well up anyway when her father switched to a slide of a new road in Nairobi. At least in Africa she hadn't been so alone. Amanda asked to be excused.

She went to her room and turned on her computer. Kevin wasn't on Facebook or Skype, so she sent him a message:

    Big dad slide show at dinner. Mucky-
    mucks. Made me miss u.

She'd forgotten about the time zones. It made her sad to think that they weren't even waking and sleeping at the same time anymore. Amanda took out her notebook to make a chart of the times she'd likely find Kevin in his room.

There was something already on the first page, some kind of writing. It must have leaked through when those rude boys in the cafeteria grabbed her notebook.

She hadn't heard what they were talking about, but the tall, spiky-haired one sure seemed excited.

Merde. Nothing was right. Even the first page of her new notebook was spoiled.

Chapter 4
Inky Gets a Warning

PRINCIPAL HAROONI GESTURED for Inky to sit down in her guest chair—a wicker chair with a long, thin back. It looked like something that might be comfortable if you were Ms. Harooni's diminutive size. The chair was one more example of why the MDA students called her "the looney." By reputation she was tough and efficient and she always dressed up as some wacky character in the annual faculty show. Inky fixed his eyes on the intricate pattern of the rug that hung over her head, a gift, no doubt, from her Iranian husband.

"Welcome to Upper School. I suppose you know why I wanted to meet you and talk to you, Michael."

No small talk here, Inky thought. It was hardly a surprise that he was seated in the principal's office. Last year his attendance was bad and his grades were worse. When he did show up, he spent most of his time in the office of the guidance counselor hearing pep talks and helping himself to the tissues and pick-me-up chocolates, neither of which made him feel better, or feel anything at all.

Principal Harooni moved her blood red glasses down her nose and turned the pages in the fat file folder opened on her desk. Inky sunk into himself, as if his lowered head could protect his heart.

"What shall we do with you, what shall we do?" she asked. "We have remedial programs when language fluency is the root of poor performance. But in your case, in your case . . ."

It was not a question she meant for him to answer, not that he could anyway. She dove into her sermonette; clearly she'd read his file. "No doubt what you've been through is a tragedy, but you must rise above. You owe it to yourself. It says that you plan to be an artist." She pointed to the file with a poppy red fingernail. "You've had ample leeway, but it has been a year and half since . . ."

She let her voice trail off meaningfully. Inky shifted in his seat. A stick of wicker poked into his butt.

What did she know of being an artist or of the "tragedy?" A sour taste filled his mouth. How was this decided, this limit to grieving? Where was this fence around before and after that even his mother was beginning to see?

His mother had sent him for "help"—group grief therapy, which didn't really help at all. The grief wasn't something Inky wanted to get over or move on from. Plus, most of the other kids in the group had lost family members to cancer after long periods of suffering. Their stories made him feel guilty in a new way. Particularly Hawk, who'd lost her mother and whose father still traveled a lot. She was quick to tease him to his face about his descent inward: the black clothes, his ever longer hair. "Get over it, Artboy," she'd say with a scowl.

He did not want to get over it, did not want to move on. That would be saying it was all right.

He'd chosen to stay in the shadows.

"And now you're in Upper School. We hold our students here to a higher standard. The degree granted from MDA is renowned all over the world. Do you know how many students we turned down for admission last year?"

It was a big speech, and Ms. Harooni's tiny frame shook with the effort of it. Her thin arms twitched, birdlike, as she gestured. Inky transformed her in his mind into a tall, thin creature with a magnificent feather hat.

His fingers itched for a pencil. He looked down to the floor to mentally place the lines on a plane. She could be his best character yet, and the thought made him smile. Drawing was the one sure thing, the only thing that mattered. Ms. Harooni waited, respectfully. He may have messed up on getting into Art & Design for high school, but he wasn't going to mess up his chance to study art in college by getting kicked out of school, as much as he wanted to tell her what he really thought of her higher standards. Inky looked up from the floor.

"Well, I seem to have made you think at least. Do you think artists are exempt from the need for a broad education? The mother lode of creativity is discipline, history and human experience. You'll find those lessons here at MDA."

He wondered if she took a special course to talk like a textbook as he looked at her cheekbones and the little jut of her chin. Ms. Harooni responded to his gaze by softening her voice. "We want you to succeed here, and expect that you'll get your grades up to par. We'll be monitoring your progress. It's time."

Inky practically raced for the cafeteria, but not to buy lunch; he hadn't adjusted to eating lunch at 11:10, and he was too angry to eat. He wanted to open his sketchbook and get right to work on his caricature of Harooni.

He longed to add a regal splash of color and thought about the oil pencils in the art room, stashed in the bin under the window that overlooked the river. The same window where his old friends had once congregated. The thought of them together in Art & Design made his stomach turn over.

"ADIP, my friend. Another day in paradise." Rungs sat down with Inky. He banged his tray so the coffee in his cup spilled over the rim. "A place of respect, that's what it says in the school charter. Lorenza should read that."

"Trouble with Lorenza? He looks cool," Inky said.

"Too cool, with his jacket and blue jeans and dreads, telling us about the core project. Social anthropology. Rules and rituals. Social structure. How people live. Says all this sitting at his desk, leaning back, and with his feet propped up. I have to hear about an assembly on learning about other cultures while looking at the bottom of his feet."

"Maybe he doesn't know it's offensive," Inky said, recalling he'd made the same mistake last year.

"Like I'm the first Buddhist he's ever had in his class." Rungs stabbed at his food, then glanced at Inky's drawing. "Hey, that's good. It's the principal, right?"

Inky was surprised that Rungs knew who the principal was. He had a way of not getting into trouble for his pranks. Last year, in middle school, he'd hacked the energy-efficient lights so that instead of turning on when students entered classrooms, they'd turn off. The prank, and the fact that no one ratted him out, gave Rungs a unique perch on the MDA social ladder. Not that he cared.

"Loony Harooni. It's a loony bird," Inky said.

"Get a warning?"

Inky nodded.

"What's the WCS?" Rungs said. "You gotta know your worst case scenario."

Rungs had a point. The worst case scenario was that he'd get kicked out of school, essentially shutting a ton of doors on his future.

He thought of Megaland and the chubby, too-bright typeface on the welcome screen. It was the entryway to his best chance, maybe his only chance, to go somewhere with his art.

Chapter 5
Amanda Signs On

SWEAT TRICKLED DOWN AMANDA'S FACE and stung the chapped edge of her lip as she ran. Finally the week was over. She loved how her muscles started to ache as her feet pounded on the pavement, so different than the packed dirt road in Nairobi. The city buildings blurred as she picked up the pace of her run. The avenues changed from names to letters of the alphabet and the big glass towers yielded to low brick buildings. She slowed to watch a group of girls jumping rope, and caught her breath before turning around and heading home. She missed running with the African kids whose marathon dreams pushed her and Derek to run ever faster. Too bad her new school didn't have a track team.

When she got home, her parents were on their way out to dinner. She could see her mother's reflection on the window, her thick orange pashmina wrapped around her shoulders. Her father stood at the door ready to go.

"I'll just microwave something," she said, seemingly to herself. Since coming to the States, Amanda had a new-found guilty pleasure. She loved frozen dinners—the ice crystals like a first snow on the vegetables and gooey cheese sauce over the chicken. Maybe the American glop would help her through the weekend's homework.

Her brain hurt from all the English—American really, not like the British English her father spoke. She struggled to understand her teachers; her last two schools were taught in French. But compared to the slang her classmates used, the writing in her textbooks was easier to understand. She looked over the handouts for her core class. They were starting with anthropology: *Social Order. Presentation of Self in Everyday Life. The Caste and Outcasts in Modern India.* Lucky her. An hour of reading about the doomed and the damned. At least she could relate.

When she was done, Amanda turned on her laptop. There was nothing fun on the Wacky World News site, and Facebook didn't appeal, either. She opened her notebook and typed in the site info that had leaked through when that Thai boy grabbed it. This would be like fieldwork, she thought.

She figured it would be a sports site, although she hadn't seen them with the soccer players. Maybe the American one was into baseball.

She was not expecting bubble type and neon colors. The "Welcome to Megaland" screen felt as homespun as baskets in a central market. Even more unexpected was the chat box that opened up.

Megaland: Hello. Welcome. What brings you to Megaland today?

Unexpected, but she liked that it was interactive. Amanda typed in "a friend."

Megaland: Good, good. Pick a screen name that reflects who you are. Are you a rocker? Like sports? Goth? Avid reader?

Amanda thought a second, looking for a word like she would among the scrabble tiles. Then she had an idea and typed,

Justagirl

Megaland: Very clever. That's a great screen name. What are your interests, Justagirl? What do you do with your friends?

The screen went blank for a moment then refreshed with the cursor positioned by her screen name in the corner. Justagirl. She liked that identity.

Justagirl: I'm new here so I don't know anyone.

Megaland: OK. What activities do you like to do with your brothers and sisters?

Justagirl: My brothers are away at school.

Megaland: OK. We can 86 that portion.

She wondered if 86 was a grade and if that was good. Or maybe there was math involved.

Justagirl: 86?

Megaland: Drop it. There are other questions in the survey.

Normally she hated the surveys that popped up on websites, but tonight she was happy to fill out a questionnaire. She was glad that someone somewhere cared what she thought. She answered the questions about her game choices; she had to think about why she liked Scrabble and avoided sites with celebrity gossip. She liked the "hot or not?" and "cool or fool?" questions. Then she faced one that stumped her.

Megaland: Anyone you're a dead ringer for?

Justagirl: what? I don't play an instrument.

Megaland: It doesn't have to be a musician, just someone you resemble.

So that was what dead ringer meant. That was another reason she hated being here. She couldn't understand what people were talking about sometimes.

The cursor blinked. She did not respond to the question.

Megaland: Is English your native language?

Justagirl: trick question. We try to speak the language of the place where we live.

Megaland: Wow. What languages do you speak?

Justagirl: French, Spanish and a little Mandarin, and English – but not New York English apparently.

Megaland: LOL. You'll pick it up, Justagirl. You sound super smart. Where are you from?

Justagirl: Another trick question. We move around a lot.

Megaland: Well, it doesn't matter. It's a small world after all and all that. You'll see that you fit in here in Megaland in ways you can't even imagine. Come back tomorrow and I'll show you how.

Chapter 6
Small Places, Big Issues

THERE WAS NO EASING into the school year with the core curriculum approach. A series of projects each trimester incorporated multiple subjects, each kicked off with both sections gathering in the auditorium. Inky plopped into his seat and took in the faded blue fabric of the curtain spanning the back of the stage. Rungs slid into the seat next to him just as Mrs. Patel began. Inky stared at Mrs. Patel's lavender dress and stoplight-red blazer, colors he thought would only be paired as the walls and trim of a room on one of those second-rate home design shows.

He'd slept fitfully, so little of what Mrs. Patel said filtered through his fuzzy morning brain. If it weren't for the air-conditioning, he was sure he'd be asleep.

". . . favorite project . . . interdisciplinary research . . . core curriculum," he heard her say. In the row in front of him, two classmates were looking at soccer stats in a carefully-folded copy of *The Guardian*.

Inky was roused to attention, though, when Mr. Lorenza added that this core project would culminate in a presentation that would constitute a major portion of their trimester grade. He did not want to have to sit in Loony Harooni's chair again.

"We'll be grading based on criteria laid out in the rubric," Mrs. Patel continued. The boys in front of Inky snickered when she said "laid." Rungs rolled his eyes.

"You'll each have a copy of the rubric to refer to as you work on your project. Do I have some volunteers to help distribute the rubric sheets?"

Ellen and Priya, two Sacred Circle girls, hopped up from their seats in the second row and distributed the papers.

Mr. Lorenza closed his attendance book and strutted halfway across the stage. "Why is social anthropology important?" He glanced around the room for impact. Papers rustled; the students were still looking over the rubric sheets. He waited until they settled down.

Inky turned his rubric page over; the blank white back was like an invitation. He reached into his pocket and felt the cool metal of his pen.

"Understanding the world means understanding the way we live together, the social order of our societies. It is the basis of the work that many of your parents do, and of the diplomatic work many of you will go on to do yourselves."

Inky stared at the blank page waiting for it to reveal what it should become. He squinted. What a funny word rubric was. As Mr. Lorenza continued his lecture, Inky started to draw. Rungs glanced at the paper in Inky's lap. Inky centered three equal squares in the middle of the page. Inside of them he wrote some of the words he heard Mr. Lorenza say: "Human condition . . . Family ties . . . Ethnicity."

"A rubric's cube," Inky wrote next to his drawing. Rungs grabbed it from him.

Mr. Lorenza paused for dramatic effect. He was the faculty advisor for the annual student play, and he tried to demonstrate dramatic flair whenever he could. "Social anthropology has been known as the investigation of more traditional or 'primitive' societies. Today, social anthropologists also study modern societies and seek out what is unique within each individual culture whilst also attempting to find the common human factor."

Inky looked suspiciously at Rungs. Even if it was a doodle, he wasn't thrilled about letting go of his drawing. Rungs fished around in his backpack and found a pencil. He held it up like a prize, which made Inky chuckle. Mrs. Patel looked in their direction. Inky put his head down and coughed.

Inky watched as Rungs drew tabs on the sides of Inky's boxes and extended some of squares. He nodded his approval. Rungs had visualized a way to make Inky's drawing 3-D.

"Now = paper cut-out," Rungs wrote. "*Rubric's Robot.*"

Mr. Lorenza finished his speech, sat down and leaned back in the chair on stage, looking satisfied with himself. He crossed his legs so the dirt-caked soles of his coffee brown leather boots faced the students. Rungs stiffened.

"No respect. He's got no respect." Inky could see his friend was seething again at the teacher's lack of knowledge of Buddhist etiquette.

Mrs. Patel recited the deadlines and required formats for the project. In her Bombay accent, she told them they needed to "state the thesis clearly, use specific examples in an original presentation on any topic within classic or modern cultural anthropology."

Inky was using the sharp point of his pen to cut around the lines. Rungs folded it into a 3-D robot and walked it across Inky's notebook. The boys behind them snorted.

Mrs. Patel gave Inky and Rungs a pointed stare. "Ooh. Show her your paper dolly," the boy behind them said.

"Let's talk about the first chapter of *Small Places, Large Issues,*" Ms. Patel said. "I know you've all done your reading."

Mr. Lorenza stood up. "Yes, what can you tell us about anthropology?"

Sven, extending his role as soccer captain, raised his hand first. "It tells us about why some people succeed in society."

Demos, in his goalie-aggressive way, called out, "It's about cultural norms, like in some cultures it's perfectly acceptable to have several wives." That got a good laugh.

Rungs raised his hand. "Respecting cultural differences by knowing what things mean in other places. Like in lots of places, it's rude to point. Or in the Philippines, calling someone over like this," Rungs said, curling his index finger, "means you think he's a dog. Or like the thumbs up sign. Here it means 'yes.' In Africa it means, 'sit on this.'" The Soccer Boys cackled and egged Rungs on.

"In Turkey, if you do this"—he made the OK circle sign—"the hole between your fingers refers to another hole." Then Rungs squared up his shoulders and looked straight at Mr. Lorenza, while his classmates gasped and laughed.

"And in Southeast Asia, and for Buddhists everywhere, it's considered rude to cross your legs when you sit down. The soles of your shoes are dirty, and to show a Buddhist the bottoms of your feet is a sign of disrespect."

The auditorium went quiet, and Mr. Lorenza let it hang for a long second. "Thank you, Mr. Rungsiyaphoratana," he finally said, pronouncing each of the seven syllables of Rungs's last name slowly and clearly. Everybody laughed—twitters of relief, more than amusement. "You certainly have a good understanding of cultural anthropology. Let's have your project begin the presentations, shall we? We'll look forward to your fascinating cultural insights."

Rungs turned over his own rubric sheet and wrote "*Pacittiya* 54 – habitual lack of respect." Inky had to look hard to make out Rung's handwriting. Had the auditorium lights dimmed, or was it because he was looking down?

Rungs outlined the letters so that they looked ominous, like something from Halloween. Inky felt a blast of air conditioning. He thought about what Rungs had written. He knew that had to do with the list of Buddhist rules to live by. And he knew it meant Mr. Lorenza was in for a lesson from his friend.

Inky shivered. He was cold, and the room really was growing darker. He heard a mechanical clack and then the soft slow whir of the screen as it started its descent in front of the auditorium.

Mr. Lorenza spoke. "Today we'll have an introduction to anthropology. One of the groups most studied by anthropologists is the Yanomami Indians. Shall we see a little film about them, Mr. Rungsiyaphoratana?"

A film? Darkness wrapped around Inky's throat, and he had to cough to breathe. A pulsing crimson color filled his head. He wasn't expecting this. He wasn't prepared for a film. He felt all clammy.

The film's narrator, in a voice of deep green velvet, said, "These Indians are oft-studied, but very much in danger. In the mid-70s, gold-diggers called *garimpeiros* started to invade the Yanomami land in the northern sector of Brazil."

The mention of Brazil started Inky's own personal film strip, the one that had been going through his head for more than a year. Spring break. Rio. Waiting in the airport. The funky purple loveseats in the TAM lounge. Candy-colored jewels in the window of H. Stern. Instead of birthday cake, Guarana soda and coconut pastries that made the waxed paper sticky. Waiting, waiting as other planes landed. His father on the way to meet them to celebrate his 13th birthday. Drawing an Indian with a bow and arrow from the tribe his father was filming. The man behind the desk with a twirly mustache saying, "*Nevoeiro.*" Fog. The hours of his birthday coming to a close. Drinking *cafezinho*, mud-dark and sweet, trying to stay up, but falling asleep on the uncomfortable chair. And then his mother's sobs. The little plane his father was in had gone down.

The lights came back up, and Inky was stunned.

"Now everyone jot down something you've learned about how environment impacts social structure," Mrs. Patel said.

Inky, clueless about the actual film, thought of an email his father had sent him from the field: "Here's something you'll like: the Awa keep the embers from their fire in a little clay pot and carry it with them to light the next one."

Chapter 7
Not a Girl in Megaland

THAT NIGHT INKY FELT PURPLE. Not the other-worldly purple of wizards and healers or the My Little Pony-purple of junior school girls, but indigo, deep indigo laced with gray. He didn't have the energy to lose himself in his art and didn't feel like watching anything on YouTube. He poked around the Internet, then clicked on the URL for Megaland.

The welcome screen looked just like when he'd first visited. He couldn't help but think how he'd change the typeface to make it more modern looking. It took a moment before anything happened. He wondered how long it would be before the real game was up and running, maybe using a welcome screen he designed.

Just as he was about to abandon the site, a large text box opened on the right side of his screen.

Megaland: Welcome back to Megaland.

When the game takes off, he's gonna have to abandon this live chat thing, Inky thought. The cursor blinked as his screen name appeared.

Picasso2B: Tnx

Megaland: Do you have some time today? We have a survey that will help determine the best role for you in the development of the Megaland site. Can you answer a few questions?

There's only one role for me, or at least only one I really want, Inky thought as he typed.

Picasso2B: K.

Megaland: Please answer all the questions as truthfully as you can. Your answers won't be shared with anyone, ever. Some of the questions may not apply to you. Don't worry. It's all part of the statistical modeling, so we can determine your areas of special insight and make this a super fun experience. Sound good?

Hell, yeah, Inky thought. This sounds legit.

Picasso2B: k

Megaland: Please check off any of the games on this list you've played in the past six months:

Gone Home
Barbie Fashion Designer
Maia
Master Chef

```
Interior Designer
Animal Doctor
Plants vs. Zombies
```

It was an odd list; no *World of Warcraft, Assassin's Creed* or *Call of Duty*. Inky checked off *Maia, Plants vs. Zombies* and *Interior Designer*. The rest seemed young and very girly. Something to do with the statistics, he figured. There probably was no need to ask about games everybody played.

The next section asked questions about his TV preferences: *The Vampire Diaries* or *Pretty Little Liars?* He passed the whole section without thinking. The TV was covered just like the mirrors, and he didn't miss it. Anything he wanted to see was online, anyway—not that he had much use for shows like *Gossip Girl*.

Megaland: Please rate the next section as "hot or not."

```
J. Crew
Angels
American Apparel
Wide leg pants
Nose piercings
Kittens
Stonewashed jeans
```

Inky stared at the screen. The list was so lame it actually made him laugh. He checked off "not" next to everything but pierced nose. A well-placed stud was hot.

Megaland: Thank you Picasso2B. Next, we have some questions about fashion preferences.

Which look do you prefer?

Smoky eye

Ruby lips

Natural neutrals

Ballroom glitz

There were images next to each choice. Good thing he read the line about some things not applying to you. Questions about costumes—swords and capes and masks—might have made sense, with the popularity of ComicCon and all, but what was up with the images that now filled his screen?

The picture accompanying "ballroom glitz" looked like a cross between a fairy princess and a sorceress, totally cheesy. He picked it anyway. If this was packaging or something for the game, he could do a whole lot better.

Megaland: Would you consider that your everyday look?

Inky hesitated a moment and reread the screen. These were some weird ass questions. No weirder than the questions the school psychologist used to ask him, he supposed, but still . . .

Picasso2B: My everyday look?????

Megaland: I know some schools limit the use of makeup.

Inky typed without thinking.

Picasso2B: makeup? WTF.

His words remained on the screen. The cursor blinked. He regretted being so harsh. Maybe this was about tolerance. He considered adding that he thought it was OK for a guy to wear makeup, but that might seem weird in another way. He just hoped he hadn't blown his chance.

Megaland: Didn't you come from the GamerGlamGirls message board? That's the code you used.

Did gamer girls who were into glamour really exist? That had to be a mighty tiny group. Inky cursed Rungs and the fancy geek girls from his computer summer camp.

He'd thought this site could be a real opportunity for him. Something to be part of. Served him right for hoping. Looked like this was just some clown selling makeup to no-life prep school princesses.

Picasso2B: I don't want to buy any makeup.

Picasso2B: I'm all about the game.

Picasso2B: Are you designing a game or not? Of course I'm not interested in buying—

The guy responded so fast Inky didn't have a chance to finish his sentence.

Megaland: MOSDEF developing a game. Sorry for the confusion, Picasso2B. No

one here will try to sell you makeup.
You don't need to wear makeup. I person-
ally think it would be better if people
would just let their true selves shine
through.

   Picasso2B: yeah and

Before Inky could finish typing, more chat appeared on his screen.

Megaland: Not only am I developing a
game, I want kids like you involved in
every stage and some especially talented
kids will get to work directly with me
one-on-one.

Inky leaned forward, as if getting closer to his
computer screen would make the words come faster. He felt the stirrings of genuine enthusiasm.

Megaland: Plus I plan to give kids
credit for their initial efforts and then
a share of the profits – which there will
be. I was successful before and I will be
again. There are enough car crash, shoot
'em up and take 'em hostage games for
boys. I want to use your special skills
to create the kind of scenarios that will
get girls excited.

Inky was sorry to see the last bit of text. A game
for girls—something else that he wasn't a part of.
Damn. But then he was never looking to play the

game, anyway. He just wanted to draw for it. He thought a moment before he typed.

Picasso2B: I'm not a girl, but I can draw things that girls like. Maybe I can draw something for you.

Swamp green desire bubbled up in him. The cursor blinked. It seemed forever before the response came.

Megaland: Well, maybe you can Picasso2B. I think I can find a special place for you here in Megaland.

Chapter 8
Loaded with Audacity

HOW APPROPRIATE, RUNGS THOUGHT as he walked towards the school gym. The recording software he was using was called Audacity. Already by the lockers he'd captured some priceless bits of that annoying Ellen Monahan saying, "Hello, Hello," and Sven saying, "Dork." During class he'd recorded several Mr. Lorenza-isms, including his signature condescension, "Shall we?" Oh, we shall. Rungs smiled at his plan.

A couple of the Soccer Boys in their shorts and shin guards nodded to him in the hall, apparently giving no thought as to why he was hanging out by afterschool soccer practice. Rungs was used to that. His classmates gave him berth like they would a big dog; respect laced with fear. Yes, he was tall and in shape, but it was more than a physical thing. His beliefs were like a protective force field around him. Beliefs that were age old and not to be tampered with, especially not by some high school teacher who should know better.

He turned on his recorder. The soccer players' grunts would be useful. The coach was having the team do pushups and crunches, mild compared to his morning Muay Thai workout. Demos finished first and pounded his chest, apelike. "Loser," he said to one of his struggling teammates. That was a keeper.

Rungs moved on to the music room. Again it was like he was invisible, hiding in plain sight. He stood in the back and let his recorder capture the sounds of the band tuning up. He walked through the music practice rooms and recorded a host of sour notes on different instruments, including a badly played euphonium, which sounded like an elephant fart. Perfect.

He paused outside of one practice room to listen to a senior girl he didn't know practicing for a recital. It was too beautiful for his purposes, but he kept taping anyway. The cello was almost as big as the girl playing it, but her notes were huge—mournful and magical. It stirred a longing in him. He missed his mother and Apsara and the ways of his village in Thailand. But as he listened to the Western melody, he also felt he might find a truly American place where he belonged.

When she finished her piece, he bowed to her and then headed home to edit his sounds.

Chapter 9
Amanda Builds Her World

"BRILLO-HEAD, BRILLO-HEAD," echoed in Amanda's brain. *Vache.* That Ellen Monahan was so horrible. This week was going no better than last.

At least she'd learned a couple of tricks from all their moving around. After dinner she unpacked the almond oil and rubbed it into her hair. The wild, dry ends did feel like a scouring pad. She twisted her brown mass of hair into a bun and wrapped a pair of her mother's torn stockings around it the way their Indonesian housekeeper had shown her.

Now to keep her head relatively still for twenty minutes. She set the Dali clock timer they'd picked up in Spain and signed on to Megaland. The screen was static for a moment as it loaded. The welcome screen teased about a new feature, "pop quiz." She settled into her chair and the chat box eventually popped up.

Megaland: Welcome back, Justagirl. I've made quite a bit of progress – there's a whole section called pop quiz. Your user-testing will be invaluable. As you take the quizzes, please ask yourself, is this a fun quiz to take? Would you recommend it? Did you learn something about yourself? Does that sound like something you can do?

Justagirl: yes

Megaland: Also, think about the premise of the game. Players complete activities to get the things they want – beautiful clothes, invites to movie premieres and fun parties, and ultimately, the pick of a dream date . . . Are you ready?

Justagirl: Sure

The text box minimized and a screen replete with quizzes popped up:

What kind of dog are you?

What type of music are you?

What city are you most like?

What's your dream guy type?

Sunset or moonlight?

Ooh, Amanda thought, it sounds like a magazine. How she loved magazines. So far, the best thing about being in New York was the Universal News shop down her street jam-packed with magazines, current ones, more magazines than Amanda had ever seen in one place. Reading them online was just not the same. In Nairobi, Amanda and her mother practically memorized their months-old copies of *Glamour* and *InStyle*.

Amanda clicked on "What kind of dog are you?" because it was the first one. Perhaps she'd do them all. The quiz came up on her screen.

```
Which best describes you?
Bubbly
Shy
Sophisticated
Quirky
```

Amanda chose "Shy" and read the next question:

```
What is your favorite thing to do on a
rainy day?
  Walk in the rain
  Go to the movies with friends
  Bake cookies
  Play games with family
```

Amanda hesitated. All her life she'd loved nothing more than playing games with her brothers. When they were stationed someplace remote, which was most of the time, games were their only amusement. Of course that was different now. Amanda was not ready to accept that change, and checked "Play games with family."

```
Choose your favorite:
Birthday cake
```

```
Sorbet
Ice cream sundae
Cookies
```

Well, birthday cake made her cringe, those too-sweet sugar flowers and everyone looking at her. Amanda chose "Ice cream sundae."

```
What kind of shopper are you?
Pick and click - online shopper
Megabrowser - visit every store in the
mall
Try, try again - bring a gazillion
things into the dressing room
Shopping??
```

Amanda laughed as she pictured the makeshift curtain you could change behind in the Nairobi market. Might as well strip before the whole town. "Shopping??" it was.

```
What do you first notice in a guy?
His looks
His clothes
His friendly smile
His eyes
```

Amanda quickly checked off the box with the word friendly. When they were in Indonesia, Derek had a Canadian girlfriend who told her all about kissing and boys. It would be fun to have a boyfriend, but she'd decided they'd have to be friends first.

```
Click for your evaluation.
```

Amanda clicked and waited for her answers, although she already knew what kind of dog she was—lost, stray.

She breathed in the deeply scented oil from her hair and looked at her not-quite olive skin, the darker side of her mother's mixed heritage. Maybe mongrel would be a better choice.

A happy puppy popped up on screen; its wagging tail made her smile.

```
You're a West Highland Terrier -
charming, stubborn and unexpectedly
brave. You're shy and have a high need
for affection. When you get it, you are
loyal and obedient.
```

That text faded and a new screen appeared.

```
Congratulations. You successfully com-
pleted a pop quiz. You may advance to
the next level. You may collect a shoe.
```

The cursor blinked in the textbox on the bottom of her screen.

Megaland: Do you like it? Was that fun?

Justagirl: yes - kind of like a magazine or like that site, Quizilla, or something you'd ask on Formspring. But I never thought of myself as a white-haired dog.

Megaland: You have dark hair?

Justagirl: very

Megaland: Do you have short legs like a Westie?

Justagirl: hardly. They called me spider legs in school.

Megaland: That sounds mean.

Justagirl: It gets worse

Megaland: Sounds like they're jealous of your assets.

That made Amanda giggle.

Justagirl: DK. My asset is pretty flat.

Megaland: Very clever, Justagirl. Lmao.

Megaland: What other quizzes would you add? The goal is to get a whole outfit and go on a date. Do you think that's the kind of thing girls want?

She thought of Ellen Monahan and the Sacred Circle girls. They were always talking about what to wear to their parties.

Justagirl: definitely

The timer she'd set earlier went off.

Justagirl: Gtg. I'll look at some magazines for quiz ideas for you.

She was anxious to rinse her hair and have it sleek and shiny. Maybe she'd wear a short skirt tomorrow to show off her long legs.

Chapter 10
Inky's Drawing Assignment

THE COLORS WERE A MASH ON THE PAGE—dark mustard, soft pumpkin, chili pepper red—as Inky attempted a design like an Aboriginal Dreaming for his core project assignment. It had worked for the school lobby; the new mural on the front wall of school had been his idea as a replacement to the so-last-century portraits of diplomats (now housed in an important closet at the UN).

Inky had envisioned it as a modern take on a Dreaming—a graphic story map of intersecting lives and places. Each day after school, his friends had sprawled out on the lobby floor, legs entangled, careful not to spill the paint palettes or Chinese takeout as they colored the lines and swirls meant to illustrate their hopes and dreams. Everyone got involved, even the soccer team, who got the concept once he explained it as "life's playbook" to them.

They'd finished it moments before the start of their middle school spring break, hours before

Inky's night flight to Rio. The breeze had mingled with the smell of paint and promise.

Now each time he entered school, the mural taunted him. The rainbow bright colors he'd picked to symbolize a world of possibility were too sharp. Garish. The colors of before.

Inky balled up the paper and tossed it across the room. He opened up a document to try to make some notes, but instead logged on to Megaland. In just a few seconds the chat box opened up, making Inky think of those annoying live help features that sometimes popped up when you were looking at electronics online. Only this time he wanted to talk.

Megaland: Picasso2B, you've returned to Megaland. Welcome back.

Picasso2B: Tnx

Megaland: Would you like to see the pop quiz section? I'm told it is reminiscent of Quizilla, which I think is good.

Picasso2B: Is that the game - a lot of quizzes?

Megaland: That's the part available for testing today.

Picasso2B: What's the point?

Megaland: Entertainment. Escape. Why do you play games?

Picasso2B: Same. How do you win?

Megaland: Complete the quizzes and games.

Picasso2B: What do they win?

Megaland: All the trappings of fame and fortune - cool clothes, hot dates.

Picasso2B: How?

Megaland: Complete the quizzes and games.

Picasso2B: Right. Got that. But how do you show it?

Megaland: I see. I see what you are after, Picasso2B. That's an element of the game I'm still working on, the graphic presentation.

Inky paused before he typed. Perfect. Sounds like there's plenty of opportunity for me.

Picasso2B: Can I help? Can I draw something?

Megaland: Can you? What kinds of things do you draw? Cartoons? Manga?

Picasso2B: Used to.

Megaland: And now?

Picasso2B: Darker stuff.

Inky caught himself; he'd best talk about skills, not tone.

Picasso2B: I'm strong with figures and perspective.

Megaland: So you're versatile. You must be very talented. Why the dark stuff?

Inky leaned back in his chair. How much did he want to share in an online convo with a stranger? But before he had a chance to look deep inside, he was typing. It was weird, but he was more comfortable with this Megaland guy than he'd been with anyone in ages.

Picasso2B: Everything changed when my father died. Quit the school paper. Quit everything really. It was like the light went out.

Megaland: Must be hard for you. How long ago?

Picasso2B: 17 months.

Megaland: That's like yesterday.

Thank you, Inky thought. Finally someone who isn't saying that I should get over it already.

Picasso2B: All I hear is it's time to move on.

Megaland: Some things you never get over.

Picasso2B: Especially when it's your fault.

Megaland: Sounds like you're blaming yourself.

Picasso2B: Can't help it. If he didn't care so much about my damn birthday he would have never been on that plane.

Megaland: Don't be so hard on yourself.

Picasso2B: I know he would have waited until the fog cleared. We had another week in Rio, he didn't have to rush.

Megaland: Want to tell me about it?

Picasso2B: IDK. I still can't believe it. He wasn't old or anything. With the things that can happen in the jungle – malaria, scorpion bites, hostile tribes

He hit some wrong keys. He couldn't focus because of the searing fluorescence of guilt.

Picasso2B: And it was my freakin birthday that did him in. He was doing great work – you know how amazing a documentary on discovering a new tribe would have been? He was there.

Megaland: Sounds like a heavy guy. And like someone who made his own decisions. Whatever went down, you have to think he made the best decision he could under the circumstances.

Those words lingered in the chat box for a moment. Inky took them in like he used to breathe in the scent of the wheaty breads his father would bake. The bright hot colors of guilt were softened by the words on the screen.

Picasso2B: That makes me feel better. Thanks for listening, or whatever.

Inky sat quietly, feeling the closest thing to peace he'd felt in ages. The chubby letters of

Megaland above the chat screen no longer bothered him. There was something homegrown and genuine about them. Then it dawned on him. This Megaland dude was speaking from experience.

Picasso2B: Sounds like you've been there

The cursor blinked.

Megaland: Not like what you've been thru, but I can relate to having your whole world snatched away and living without what you love.

Inky wanted him to say more and started typing, but before he could get his words out, he saw the offer he'd been hoping for.

Megaland: So. Drawing. Are you up to trying some drawings for Megaland?

Inky pumped his fist in the air.

Picasso2B: Mos def. What do you want?

Megaland: I could use some art for the Dream Date segment. There'll be a main guy - well-built, good hair, rock n roll look, the kind girls like. Also a biz guy close-cropped hair, suit jacket. Then a couple of others, a sports type, hipster, lots of different facial looks, different eyes, nose, skin color. All friendly smiles. The kind of guys you'd want to know, that make girls feel comfortable. Does that make sense?

Picasso2B: I can picture it.

Well, maybe not the stuff that girls liked.

Megaland: Excellent. And if you do a good job, maybe I'll have you draw the girl. So far I'm thinking dark hair, long legs and not too curvy, if you know what I mean.

Chapter 11
A Muse Emerges

THE CAFETERIA WAS UNUSUALLY QUIET; the whole grade was working on their outlines for their core presentations. Even Rungs was hyper-focused, reviewing lines of code on his mini-computer, although Inky wasn't sure what that had to do with his report on Buddhist practices.

Inky was pleased with the drawings he'd done the previous night—kind of a cross between a men's fashion photo spread and the old dancer iPod commercials. He looked them over and knew he should be thinking about ways to make them work for his project, too, but all he could think about was creating the girl character for Megaland. It was always easier to draw if he had a real person as a starting point. Rungs looked up as Inky was staring at the Sacred Circle's table.

"You're not thinking about the dance?"

Inky shook his head. "No way." He was so not ready for a school dance.

"Oh, I get it," Rungs said, stealing a glance at Inky's open sketchbook. "Your project. You're drawing social structure."

"Social structure. Yes, social structure," Inky said, trying not to let on that he still didn't know what to say about the drawings. "Thank you for seeing that." His excitement made him speak loudly enough for the new girl at the little table behind them to look up.

"Chill. The new girl is staring at you," Rungs said.

Inky could feel his cheeks turning red. He angled to look at her, taking in her long, heart-shaped face and amber eyes. She turned her head and her ponytail swayed.

"Her name's Amanda. I have core classes with her," Rungs said.

The overhead light caught the tiny diamond in her nose and made a rainbow that Inky thought was meant just for him. Inky smiled at her, his mind like a camera taking a picture that he'd work from later.

He'd found his secret muse for the next drawing for Megaland.

Chapter 12
Rungs Sounds Off

RUNGS WALKED BEHIND THE ROWS of desks to the computers in the back of the room. He nodded to Demos, who was updating his Facebook status. Demos looked up guiltily.

"It's cool," Rungs said.

He stood by the computer that was connected to the classroom whiteboard and typed in some code. He chuckled to himself over the irony that his classmate was feeling guilty.

Rungs popped a flash drive in to the side of the machine and glanced around to observe his classmates entering the room. Demos continued typing.

No one looked at Rungs as he restarted the computer. He felt satisfied as he heard the winch-winch noise that meant his program was loading. He went to his seat and strained to hear the sound of the computer over his classmates' chatter. When the computer became quiet, he picked up his water bottle as if he needed to refill it, and headed to the classroom door. He paused by the computer and stealthily palmed his flash drive and shut down the computer.

He stepped outside and walked down the hall to fill his water bottle. He let the flash drive slip into the water fountain and watched the water dribble on to it. Revenge would be sweet. Lorenza disrespected his customs; now he'd get a taste of how that offense, a *Pacittiya*, was dealt with.

When his bottle was full, he recapped it and picked up the now ruined flash drive and tossed it in the trash. "Leave no traces," his father would say.

When Rungs returned to his seat, Mr. Lorenza was standing in front of the classroom. "Are we ready?" he said as he waited for the class to turn in his direction.

Rungs had a hard time concentrating on the lecture. He was imagining how his carefully recorded sounds would be triggered from the computer.

Mr. Lorenza sat down at his desk and grabbed the clicker. He leaned back. Rungs felt his shoulders tighten. But instead of bracing for the affront of Lorenza's feet on the desk, Rungs smiled at the thought that his recordings were now loaded on the classroom computer.

"Let's have a look on the white board, shall we?" Mr. Lorenza put one foot up on the desk, then another. "Could someone turn on the computer?" he said.

The ever-helpful Priya volunteered. Rungs listened as the computer started up, sensing the extra few seconds it took to load the new program.

Of course he'd be suspected. But as long as there were no witnesses, there'd be no way to trace it to him. The flash drive was trashed, and even if someone could recreate his program, he'd left no signature on the files.

Rungs expected Mr. Lorenza to put the rubric up on the whiteboard. He'd read each point to the class because it was an opportunity to use the inflections of his well-trained former actor's voice to emphasize the required elements. Ego.

Then, Rungs figured, when Lorenza was ready to have the students present their project ideas, he'd call on them by displaying their names on the whiteboard screen. Mr. Lorenza liked to stage direct.

Rungs knew he'd be called on first because of his comments in the auditorium. He planned that the first sound triggered by the first click of the controls was the sound of the wind, a gentle hush. Rungs bowed his head when Mr. Lorenza called his name— he used the gesture of humility to hide his smile. He heard the subtle rustle of leaves in the wind.

Rungs stepped up to the front of the room. He had no notes. "My project will be about *buat phra*, becoming a monk, something most Thai men do before they are married. It's a rite of passage and a way to get closer to nirvana by studying Buddha's teachings.

"It's not a forever thing," Rungs continued. "Usually it lasts for one *phansa*, the three-month rainy season that starts in July. In my village, all the boys over 16 become monks together, and then there's a giant ordination ceremony. It's the biggest party of a guy's life."

Rungs thought about beautiful Apsara back in Thailand and almost lost his train of thought. Right after his *buat phra*, he planned to ask her to marry him.

He looked over at Mr. Lorenza, who was starting to lean back in his chair. "My project will talk about the monk's vows, the 227 laws. I'll focus on a couple of them: *adhikarana-samatha*, or the settlement of issues; the non-doing of all evil; and the doing of what is skillful."

Rungs looked directly at Mr. Lorenza. "Of course, you do not have to wait to keep your heart and body pure and lead a life in accordance with the teachings of the Buddha."

"Well, well, Mr. Rungsiyaphoratana, we've learned much here. I'll remind you that you need to use a multidisciplinary approach for your project. Find a way to illustrate some of those customs or principles."

"Oh, I hear you, Mr. Lorenza. I've already started on that," Rungs said.

Mr. Lorenza clicked the controller to bring up the next name on the screen and read, "Helen Stegmann."

"Dork, dork," Sven was heard saying.

Mr. Lorenza looked toward the Soccer Boys' row. "We'll show the courtesy we'd want for ourselves." Sven shrugged and looked around for support, but found no sympathy. They'd all heard Sven's voice, and no one dared to call Hawk a dork.

Rungs had a hard time not smiling. The timing worked out even better than he had planned. He concentrated on his breathing, and wished that Inky was in his class so they could share in the moment. He heard nothing of what Hawk said, but clapped politely when she was finished.

The sound of a squeaky violin accompanied the slide with the name Amanda Valdez Bates. Rungs was glad it wasn't the euphonium. She looked nervous enough.

Mr. Lorenza seemed to think the sound was the squeak of a chair and looked over to the Soccer Boys' row with a warning glance.

Amanda spoke about always being new and re-lating to gypsies and Arabs and nomads. She rocked from foot to foot when she spoke. She had her thick hair pulled back. It reminded Rungs of a swishing horsetail and it made him a little dizzy. Her thoughts were equally confounding. Some-thing about being a fast runner and how she'd like to do her project on running and not knowing where to call home.

Mr. Lorenza seemed uncomfortable with her discomfort and cut her off. "I appreciate that your subject matter is heartfelt, but I'm not sure I can find the theme in there. In our core studies at MDA, we emphasize organization and focus."

Rungs watched her tap her foot as the teacher spoke. She leaned forward like she was in a starting block, and Rungs half expected her to take off.

"I think that since you're new, it would be interesting for you to study MDA as a microcosm. You can look at social structure, group behavior, multiculturalism, or even the role of sports. You decide how you want to fine-tune it. It'll give you a good excuse to get to know everyone." Mr. Lorenza saw how dejected she was and added, "I'll assign someone to help you."

Then the teacher dove into a monologue about the assignment and the due date. The class was quiet. While he talked, he clicked his remote to show a blank screen, which triggered the next of the sounds.

It was Demos' voice saying, "Loser." Mr. Lorenza's face contorted in anger. Several students gasped and the braver ones looked over in the direction of Demos and the Soccer Boys.

Rungs sat back in his chair, put one foot up on his desk and prepared to savor his retribution.

Chapter 13
Class, Caste and Costume

IN THE NEIGHBORING CLASSROOM, Mrs. Patel called on Inky. He took his time gathering his sketches.

"My topic is social structure in modern American culture." He paused a moment. "I plan to present my project as a series of images." As soon as he touched the thick paper of his sketches, he felt better, like a toddler with his favorite blanket. "Here's what I have so far."

Inky held each picture up to the class, making sure to first show them to Mrs. Patel. His classmates were quiet. His drawings were good and fun to look at, particularly the guy on the lime-colored Vespa with the forest green leather man-bag slung across his body. Another image, created for Megaland, was the grinning rocker dude, microphone in hand, clad in skinny, skinny ink-black leather jeans and an old-school shag haircut. The girls seemed to like that one.

When he'd shown all the pictures, Inky turned to Mrs. Patel, hoping she would find his effort acceptable. "Well, that's as far as I've gotten, but I'll work on it some more."

"Thank you, Michael," the teacher said. "I'm glad to see you've been working on your project. You need to clarify your area of exploration. I expect you to have an overview and a thesis statement. Do you have the rubric?"

He pictured the rubric robot and smiled. "Yes, Mrs. Patel. Thanks. I'll be sure to look at it." He'd hoped that was it, and she'd send him back to his seat.

"Perhaps you'll want to base your final presentation on 'Class, Caste and Costume.' You'll find that chapter in your reader. See if it doesn't inform your project."

* * *

That night Inky worked on his sketches, sharpening lines, adjusting angles and cursing himself for his foray into abstract art last year, then remembering exactly why realism had been overwhelming.

He added tattoos to the arm of a basketball player and etched "Megaland" into the character's hair in the same bubble typeface as the welcome screen. He toyed with drawing a soccer player, but he hated the thought of spending any of his time thinking of kids he detested.

He put a couple of new lines down; the torso he drew was long and slender. He penciled in lines for arms and legs, then elongated them to suggest a runner's body. He stared at the page for a moment to let it suggest a direction.

This was definitely a girl's body, long, lean and elegant. He draped her in a cropped jacket, rounding the area under the arms to give her more shape. He sketched pants with a wide flared leg and buttons across a tight waist. Then he worked on the features, shaping the face of his drawing with the same heart shape as Amanda's. He added a small dot to the left side of her nose.

He stepped back and thought about the hair. It had to be dark, yes, but he wanted to do something dramatic, something different. His hand was ahead of his brain, and he drew an asymmetrical line ending at the top of the left cheekbone. He made the part jagged, then shaped it like a lightning bolt. On the right side he drew in some bangs. They were more like a fringe, with the pieces tickling the brow and longer pieces kissing the nape of the neck. It was hip and sophisticated and totally original.

With his colored pencils, he made the pants slate gray and the jacket black with purple stitching, and colored a line that suggested a bright yellow shirt underneath. He added purple streaks to the bangs and a smudge of purple on the eyes and lashes.

Inky set all of his Megaland sketches out on the floor. One by one he scanned his sketches into a program that transformed them into a more usable file. When he was satisfied, he signed on to Megaland. While he was waiting for the chat box to appear, he noticed there was no "contact us" tab. He guessed it was because it was a beta site.

Megaland: Welcome back, Picasso2B.

Picasso2B: I have those drawings for you. Where can I send them?

Megaland: Drawings for me? Now? This is exciting, but unexpected.

The cursor blinked for a moment. Inky wondered why it was unexpected. Did he think he'd flake out?

Megaland: It'll take me a little time to set up an inbox for you to upload to. Could you come back for instructions tomorrow?

Inky was disappointed. He wanted quick props for his work.

Picasso2B: I'd really like to know what you think. Is there someplace I can email them?

Megaland: My email can't accept attachments. Viruses and all. Let me see if I can scare up the IT guy. He's usually pretty close to his computer. Check in later tonight.

Picasso2B: K.

Even though he typed that it was OK, it really wasn't. This guy seemed pretty buttoned up in the beginning with his research questions. What was up with not having an FTP site or some kind of file sharing? Even MDA had that. Maybe he was still in the research phase or something. Whatever. What mattered was that the Megaland guy liked his work enough to use it in the game.

Later that night Inky signed on again and got instructions for sending his images. He whistled as he uploaded his files, made himself a snack and returned to Megaland. The dialogue box popped up immediately. Which made him wonder, didn't the guy have a life? Even his mother took a break from work once in a while to go out for dinner with friends. But Inky abandoned that thought as soon as he saw the comment about his artwork.

Megaland: Picasso2B, you are a wonderful artist. I couldn't be more excited to have the opportunity to work with you. It is truly a happy accident that brought you to me. I can anticipate many uses for your talents.

Yes. Inky wanted to screen-capture that chat and save it. But first he had to reply.

Picasso2B: Really glad u like them. I'm very interested in graphics for games.

Megaland: Makes sense because you have a real talent. I think you have a natural understanding of story development, and that's something you don't always find in an artist.

Picasso2B: Thanks. That makes me happy. Now I have to make the drawings work for my school project. And I'm nowhere with that.

Megaland: What's the topic?

Picasso2B: Class, caste and costume.

Megaland: Pretty advanced stuff. I'll have to look for identifying marks in your sketches. That's the thing with caste right? The marking that tells everyone where you stand.

Inky liked the way this dude told him something he probably should have known. It was the way his really good art teacher last summer would show him things. The way his father used to help him with his homework.

Picasso2B: I have to read some essay, then figure it out.

Megaland: Sounds to me like you'll be good to go once you focus on it.

Picasso2B: that's the thing. It's hard to concentrate. All this stuff in my head gets in the way.

Megaland: I think I know what you mean - the what ifs, the movie that won't turn off.

Picasso2B: yup. And memories. There are things I can't shake.

Inky thought of a photograph from some insurance papers his mother filed. A patch of land, perhaps one the pilot had thought would make a good spot for an emergency landing. Everything was charred, bits of baggage, pieces of the plane.

Megaland: Anything in particular?

Picasso2B: It's stupid maybe but in this picture of the crash site, I think I see some of my father's stuff.

The cursor blinked. It felt polite, like the guy was giving him space to say stuff or not.

Picasso2B: I swear I can see his mangled camera and a thin metal razor like the one he used. I see it in my head all the time.

Megaland: For me it's a smell. Loss, ruin - they stink. I can't shake the smell - guys too close, too constant.

Inky wondered if he was talking about maybe being on the road with a band or something.

Megaland: That, and I gotta know what time it is. I can't sleep. Like I'll miss something good. Drives me crazy how much I missed when I was away.

He was curious where the Megaland guy had been. But before he could think much about it, there was more on the screen.

Megaland: Forget that. Forget about me. You were saying there were things you can't shake . . .

Picasso2B: I wonder what it must have been like when the plane started to go down. How did the scenery look? Did it whiz by? Did he think of us? When was it exactly? When I was in the hotel getting ready to go to the airport, sitting by the AC and eating strange fruit?

Megaland: So much you'll never know. So much to regret. But we can't dwell in the past. We must move forward. And our forward, Picasso, my man, is Megaland.

Picasso2B: Does that mean you'll use my drawings in the game?

Megaland: It's quite possible. Of course, everything is market-tested.

Picasso2B: I have another sketch - it's of a girl.

Megaland: Do send it. I believe I'll find many ways to use your work.

Chapter 14
Green Goddess

IN THE CAFETERIA, AMANDA'S FACE was flushed like she'd been running. She was embarrassed by her presentation and that she'd been assigned a topic. And the topic she'd been assigned—*quelle barbe*—so annoying. If Mr. Lorenza was even one millimeter more approachable she might talk to him, but he was so smug and full of himself, she doubted he'd change his mind.

She pushed her way past the taco station, inadvertently bumping into Ellen Monahan.

"Watch it, Spider Legs."

Amanda ignored her and asked for a grilled cheese.

Amanda looked at the perfect little flip in Ellen's hair; her presentation would be polished. Amanda had always done well in school, but she was used to studying and tests, not projects and presentations.

Well, she wasn't going to wallow. She tried to keep her thoughts on the salty, gooey orange cheese on sweet white toast. She'd just have to learn how to speak in front of a group.

Amanda selected the vegetables for her side salad and headed to the little table in the back of the cafeteria where she'd been sitting alone since the start of school. It was taken; two students were seated in front of a pile of flyers about the school clubs.

She sat at the table where the Thai boy was sitting by himself. His presentation in class made her think he wasn't as rude as he seemed that first day. She put her tray down at the edge of the table. Amanda put her elbows down to her sides and pressed her palms together below her chin. She bent her head slightly. The prayer-like gesture was called *wai*—their old housekeeper had taught her the greeting. It was a sign of respect in Thailand. The boy smiled at her and seemed surprised.

"Lived in Laos once," Amanda said.

While Rungs introduced himself, one of the students at the club table called out, "The UNICEF club is planning a haunted house."

Amanda saw Rungs's friend walking towards them. A couple of the boys in soccer shirts snickered. "Of course, some of us already *are* a haunted house," the thick black-haired one said.

"NRN," Rungs said as his tall friend sat down. "No response necessary."

The boy nodded to Rungs, then looked at her. She could tell by the red patches on his neck that he was really embarrassed about being teased. It happened to her all the time when she didn't know what to say. Like now.

Rungs looked down under the table at some device.

Amanda stabbed at her lettuce. The boy ate his sandwich without saying a word. She looked up at the clock. She thought she felt him looking at her, but when she glanced over he was looking at a thin slice of tomato that had slipped out of his sandwich.

Another fifteen minutes until lunch was over. Not enough time to go for a run. She could go up to the roof with the view of the East River, but she didn't want to stand alone. She tried that last week and felt like she was out on the open plain, exposed, like some kind of small bush animal.

She snuck a glance at the boy. He was looking at his tomato like it was the most interesting thing in the world. She knew that look. How many times had she pretended to be interested in something as a buffer to the world?

The lettuce trembled on her fork. She hoped he didn't notice.

"The dressing is good," she said to him.

"Never tried it," he said, at least looking up from his tomato.

"I'm Amanda. I'm new."

"Michael. But everyone calls me Inky." She liked his long, scraggly hair and dark-gray nervous eyes. His discomfort made her feel more at ease.

"Enqui? What language is that?"

"No, Inky. Like pen and ink."

"How'd you get that name?"

Amanda felt proud of herself. Her mother always told her that the way around shyness was to express interest in the people around her by asking questions.

He hesitated before he answered her, like he was filling himself up with resolve. She did the same thing before she spoke to people.

"I always loved to draw—especially with my father's fountain pen. He used emerald green ink," he said, suddenly more animated. "I loved how heavy that pen felt in my hand. The swirls of color on its casing made me think of an ice cream sundae when everything melts in the bowl."

"I know those pens. Like Venetian paper." Amanda thought she saw him pat his pocket.

"Right. So one day I was sitting in the big wooden chair at my father's desk drawing a birthday card. My father was printing some pictures. He made the bathroom into a darkroom and I couldn't open the door while he was working or his film would get ruined."

"A photographer, wow," Amanda said.

"Filmmaker, actually." He stopped and seemed to get lost inside his head.

"So. Your nickname?"

"Yeah, right. Sorry. I was drawing a card, and the pen ran out of ink. When I tried to change the cartridge, I made a huge mess and got ink all over my hands."

Amanda nodded for him to continue.

"I didn't wash it off too well and I went to the birthday party with green hands. Hawk, well, she was Helen then, was Little Miss Manners and shook my hand and said they were dirty."

Amanda took another bite of salad, careful not to drip dressing on her shirt.

"She thought it was funny or something when I told her it was ink and yelled out to everyone, 'Inky, Inky, Inky.' Even then she had that thing that makes people follow. All the kids at the party—basically everyone in our class—mimicked her. From then on, I was Inky. Inky Kahn."

Amanda saw Inky's cheeks flush. "Wow." He was cute when he was embarrassed, in a gangly sort of way. "Great story. Did you like the nickname?"

"Well, it fit. That's the thing about Hawk. Plus, I didn't want to be a wet blanket."

Amanda didn't know what he meant about the blanket. She pointed to the remnants of her salad. "This dressing really is good. Green Goddess." She thought of a silly joke her brother once told her at a restaurant and thought she'd try it. "Maybe you know. What Greek goddess is the goddess of lettuce?"

Amanda regretted it as soon as she said it. What a lame remark. But miraculously, he smiled, and even laughed a little, making the bite of sandwich give him a bit of trouble. That made her smile.

But Inky's laugh stopped abruptly. Amanda wondered what stopped him.

"Hey, new girl," she heard someone say behind her.

Inky grabbed his tray like he was ready to go. Amanda turned to see the girl who presented before her in Mr. Lorenza's class.

"We were just talking about you," Inky said. The girl snorted.

"So, new girl. I've been assigned to help you with that lame-ass project Lorenza stuck you with. Call me Hawk. Like Tony Hawk."

Amanda wondered why she'd glared at Inky. She couldn't read his expression, but it seemed like a dark cloud passed over his head. Hawk wagged her finger for Amanda to come with her. She didn't want to leave, but Inky was right, Hawk was like a magnet; she had something that made it impossible to say no to her.

"I can give you the story on everyone. This is your lucky day." Hawk shot a glance at Inky and Rungs.

Amanda felt neither relieved nor lucky. But she needed Hawk's help with the project.

"First, don't sit with them." Hawk pointed to the table where Amanda had been sitting. "Also, don't sit at the nut table."

"The nut table?"

"Yeah. That's where they used to put the kids who brought lunch that had nuts in it. The nut allergy thing. They tried to make us a no-nut school, but the Africans and south Asians protested that peanut oil and peanuts were a cultural right. So they set up the nut table. Only now it has nothing to do with the lunch you eat, if you get what I mean."

"Oh," Amanda said. "They seemed nice to me."

Hawk shot her a look. "Things are not what they seem at MDA," she said as the bell rang. "I'll meet you after school," Hawk called out. She sounded so tough when she said it, Amanda wasn't sure if it was a threat or a promise.

Chapter 15
The Nth Factor

"YOU LIVE IN THE NTH FACTOR? The Nth Factor? I'm totally walking you home," Hawk said as Amanda took her books out of her locker. Amanda couldn't imagine what could be appealing about the building she'd begun to think of as the ice house.

"The slope of the plaza is ridiculous." When Amanda didn't reply Hawk added, "Guess you don't skate."

On the walk to Amanda's building, Hawk talked about skateboards, which Amanda understood no better than the stuff Hawk was telling her about their classmates. Was Priya the tall one or was that Shiri? Amanda tried to memorize the stories in the same way she'd learn a new language or neighborhood each time they moved.

"So I have to fill you in on everyone. The host country kids—that's MDA speak for 'our parents live in New York'—we've been together since junior school. The international kids come and go—like you. How long you think you'll be here? Two years?"

"My dad really likes his new job."

"OK. Then you'll stay through high school— Upper School, we say. So you better listen up, 'cause there's stuff you gotta know. Everybody does." Hawk hopped on her skateboard, got up some speed, then jumped up while the board turned around under her.

She landed on the board, right in front of Amanda. "You know Ellen?"

Quelle bitch, Amanda thought, but didn't say. She rolled her eyes. "She's in core class with me."

"I know. She can be pretty rough."

"She's your friend."

Hawk nodded.

"Your best friend?"

"You can't really be besties with Ellen. The only thing she really cares about is appearances." Hawk snorted. "And her mother. She worships her moth-er—that's her best friend.

"So her parties—all the cute guys go. Alonzo, who graduated a couple of years ago, he's an un-derwear model now. Shiri was going out with him last year . . . until Ellen's mother got into his un-derwear, shall we say."

"What? No," Amanda said.

Hawk took off on her skateboard, this time jumping up and grabbing her board as she landed. "Oh, yeah."

"How horrible. And you said she worships her mother. How can that be?"

"Her mom got Ellen and Priya and Shiri walk-ons in a TV pilot through his agent, and took Ellen to Paris for a new wardrobe—after it made Page Six."

Amanda wondered about page six. Was that like 86? What was it with these Americans and their numbers for things? She'd have to look that one up, too.

"She didn't care so much about Alonzo, anyway. He was going to dorky Hofstra."

Hawk skated up and back, leaving Amanda with thoughts of her own mother. It was like they were from different worlds, starting with their looks. Amanda was all straight lines to her mother's soft round curves.

"See," Hawk said, as they arrived at the Nth Factor plaza. "The perfect mini skate park—out of the view of the doorman, and no one who lives here ever sits on the benches." A couple of older, tough-looking skateboarders were already there. They all waved to Hawk, who greeted them by flicking her skateboard with her foot so that it spun underneath her while she was in the air.

Hawk circled the perimeter of the park, jumped over a low curb, then balanced on the edge of the tiers of the concrete that formed a sitting area.

"Sick," one of the skater boys called out.

Amanda sat on a bench and watched Hawk pick up speed as she circled. At the end of the spiral, she popped her board so she was suspended in air hovering above her skateboard. As she came down, her front foot almost missed the board. Amanda saw Hawk look to see if the other skateboarders had seen her wobble.

"Need a break," she said as she plopped on the bench next to Amanda.

"Do you always ride without a helmet? Isn't that dangerous?"

Hawk sneered and tugged her blonde ponytail out of the back of her shirt. "I never fall, and big whoop if I did. Like there's anyone who'd care. Haven't you ever done anything dangerous?"

She wasn't sure if Hawk was looking for a response. The question made Amanda think of the riots after the election in Nairobi and how they snuck out of town, driving past the avenue of Jacaranda trees filled with big menacing birds. Was it dangerous? Daddy seemed in control, but she knew it was dangerous because of the look on her mother's face. She'd said, "I love you, I love you," and shoved a paper with emergency addresses and phone numbers into the pocket of Amanda's jeans.

Amanda sensed that if she had a good story for Hawk they might be friends. But like so many things, it was all daddy and her brothers. She wanted to tell something of her own.

"Well. Have you?"

"One time in Indonesia," Amanda said, "the housekeeper's daughter and I snuck under the fence and played in the remains of a hotel that'd been destroyed in the tsunami."

Hawk looked down to her skateboard. "That's cool, I guess," she said, sounding like she meant it.

Amanda felt relieved. *At least she doesn't think of me as a complete wimp.* Right then, Amanda resolved to be braver. She smiled at Hawk.

"I haven't traveled much. My father does enough of that for all of us," Hawk said.

"What about you? I bet you've done all kinds of brave things," Amanda said.

"The whole time my mother was sick, I guess. It was me who took care of her," Hawk said, rolling her skateboard back and forth under her foot. "Mostly I'd curl into bed with her after school and tell her about my day. Sometimes she understood and sometimes she was all doped up and just drooled. So every day was brave."

Amanda had been expecting to hear something boy-brave and was surprised when Hawk continued.

"The bravest thing? Maybe the bravest thing was when she died. My father was in Switzerland—some bank thing—he's a big deal . . ." She stopped herself. "It doesn't matter who he is. He was away and my mother died. At home. I knew she was dead and I sat with her and held her hand. And then I cleaned her up and put her in a pretty dress before I called anyone."

Amanda reached out for Hawk's hand and stroked it. She didn't know what to say, but the silence felt deep, not strained.

"Thanks for not saying anything," Hawk said after a minute. "Most people say stupid stuff."

Chapter 16
Between the Lines

INKY REALLY HAD TRIED TO STUDY for the science quiz, but he kept thinking about lunch with Amanda. He hated that she'd heard him being teased, but she was nice to him anyway.

That didn't do him any good now on the quiz, which asked him to compare and contrast how plants and animals differ beyond basic life functions. He stared at the blank space for his response. His fingers took over, and he started drawing. First he drew a carrot growing underground, then he sketched a sunflower turned towards the sun.

On the opposite side of the paper, Inky drew an Indian in a loincloth with a bow and arrow raised and aimed at a jungle cat. He knew he needed more, knew that he needed to write an essay, and that not writing it meant another visit with Looney Harooni. Inky wasn't stupid. He knew he was supposed to write about how humans used tools, about how humans were different because of planning and intent. He just couldn't express it in words.

When the final bell rang, he raced out of school, not even waiting for Rungs. He needed a change of scenery, so he headed to an atrium in a Madison Avenue office building he'd discovered on his way home from his summer art classes. The lobby had an indoor wall of water, some small café tables and really good light. Inky found a seat among the out-of-work businessmen, the homeless and some stray tourists.

He opened his sketchbook to work on his school project. Looney Harooni would want to see it. He still liked his drawings, but he didn't know what to say about them. He wrote down some phrases: "Ways a man can be. Clothing is costume. A way that people judge one another. How people show themselves to the world."

It was all so obvious. It was all such bull. Inky put his head down and let himself be mesmerized by the trickle of water. His project was going nowhere and he knew it. He looked around him—the homeless and the jobless. Lost souls. He fit right in.

When he got home, he found some money and a note from his mother: "I have a date. I might be late. Do not fret, be sure to get a good night's sleep." Even her notes sounded like marketing copy. She'd know what to write about his drawings, but she wasn't home—as usual.

Inky pocketed the money. The note made him lose his appetite. Right before school started, he'd heard her talking with her friend Gloria from work. September was her new start. She said she'd turned the corner and had posted her profile on Match.com. Inky had barely spoken to her since.

He wondered if a computer would ever have matched her up with his father. They'd met through his mother's job. The big pharmaceutical company she worked for had been skewered in the news about the high price of its drugs.

She'd suggested they provide free vaccines to poor people in Brazil—and film it. She hired his dad, an anthropologist/filmmaker specializing in South America. When his dad told the story of how they met, he'd say, "She called it corporate social responsibility and needed me for credibility. I called it propaganda and needed the money." No, no computer would've put them together.

"Turning the corner." Her words, and Looney Harooni saying, "It's time," echoed in his head. He didn't want to think what her date was like. The floor creaked. "Some of us *are* a haunted house." Demos's words. He retreated to his room and crawled into the space below his bed. He needed a dose of unreality, and a little understanding. He signed on to Megaland.

Megaland: Hello again, Picasso2B. How is our resident artist? What brings you back today?

Inky liked how that sounded, resident artist. He supposed it meant his last drawings must have been acceptable.

Picasso2B: Taking a break from homework.

Megaland: I'm just finishing up some new modules - more of the dating sequence and a mini game on visual puns. I'd love to know what you think of it as an artist. Btw, why Picasso? Your work is more realistic.

Picasso2B: The school admissions officer said it about me to my dad. They put all the kids applying to kindergarten in a room and had them draw. They looked at mine and said I was "a regular Picasso to be." Makes a good username.

Megaland: Indeed. They were right. You are a talented artist. Where will you train?

The mud colors in Inky's mind lightened.

Picasso2B: IDK. Didn't have the grades to get in to the special high school. I messed up pretty bad last year.

Megaland: That's too bad. Your talent should be nurtured. Can you reapply? Or find another school?

Inky appreciated that here was an adult who wasn't telling him what he had to do, but was asking him about alternative plans—even if he wasn't ready to admit that *this* was his Plan B.

Picasso2B: It was a one-shot. I blew it.

Megaland: I messed up once, too. But now it's time for a comeback. I'm gonna make Megaland a big success. Phoenix rising and all that. You can too.

Picasso2B: not likely. I blew it at school and my friends are gone. Everything sucks.

Megaland: Like a light was turned off and you're left alone in the room?

Picasso2B: exactly that.

Inky again had the sense that the Megaland dude was talking about himself. He wondered if he should ask, or say nothing. This guy seemed pretty open to sharing, and their conversations made him feel better.

Picasso2B: how do you know? You seem pretty together.

Inky wondered what the guy on the other end was like. Maybe he should ask him which of his drawings he most resembled. The cursor blinked. He was beginning to think it was wrong to ask when text started to appear.

Megaland: I had it all once – a happening New York recording studio booked 24/7. Gold records on the wall, a smart, pretty wife, great apartment. Like the movies.

Picasso2B: Sweet

Megaland: Then the world changed. The digital revolution. Home studios. Everybody was a producer. In a couple of years I lost it all - the apartment, the wife. Dark times. I can't even tell you how dark. This game – it's my chance to rise again.

Inky so totally understood. He could feel the regret and the hope. It stirred up feelings inside of him. All the times in grief therapy when they'd gone around in the circle, they were supposed to say how they were feeling. Hawk could always come up with some angry emotion. But into the second year, Inky was still numb. "Tell us what you're feeling now," the leader would say, but there were no words, only colors, and they were all muddy, like the mix of colors in the runoff wash on his palette at the end of the day.

Megaland: And maybe it'll be your chance too. No more darkness. A bright new path. We'll make this game rock. Nothing's better than success. Whatd'ya say? You in?

Inky sucked in his breath. In three words this guy got it. No more darkness.

Was he in? Did the sun rise in the east in a cool mute of color? There was never anything Inky wanted more to be a part of.

Picasso2B: In all the way. I can draw anything you want.

Megaland: Thank you, Picasso2B. I think you will be a great asset. You can call me Woody, since we're working together and all. Hey, do you want to check out the new parts of the game?

Picasso2B: Save that for the real testers. I feel like drawing now. Good night, Woody.

Megaland: Good night, Picasso2B.

Inky felt the green of spring buds. He took out his colored pencils and started to sketch.

He recreated the face and body of the girl he'd drawn for Megaland, the girl based on Amanda. He thought of her at the cafeteria table, smiling her shy smile. There was something so natural about her.

Inky swatted a straggle of hair away from his face, scrunched up his eyes and tried to conjure up the exact green of the iceberg lettuce in Amanda's bowl. He concentrated as if everything depended on it.

He wanted his drawing of her to be perfect, and focusing on the right shade helped. He knew he was rusty. The caricatures for the school newspaper and quick sketches of his friends, that was before. Last year he filled his notebooks with abstracts, a mad rush of color, emotion running like muck. Rivers of his guilt traversing the page in each mad drawing.

He started working on her hair. He sketched a string of leaves flowing down toward her shoulders. Then he tucked a broccoli flower behind her ear.

For her dress he made a gown of lettuce and spinach leaves. He hummed as he shaded them. It was an elegant dress, and his character looked truly lovely.

There were definitely peas in her salad. He remembered how Amanda balanced one on her fork while she laughed (she laughed!) at his story about how he got his nickname. And asparagus? Did she have asparagus? Are there even asparagus in October?

The top of his chest throbbed as if his heart had been pushed up, displaced by grief, his insides swollen from the burden he carried. He bit his lip as he struggled to recall the items on her lunch tray.

Inky gave her some final ornamentation: an asparagus spear twisted around her neck and some delicate pea earrings. None of his pencils were quite the right color for the earrings. He wanted a brighter green. He knew just the color—the ink his father had used.

Inky hesitated. He'd last been in his father's study to help collect slides for the memorial ceremony his father's colleagues had put together. When it was done, they'd shut the door and had avoided that side of the apartment ever since.

He wanted to impress the game developer; this was his shot at having his art used. And if this worked, maybe it wouldn't matter so much that he wasn't going to art school with his friends. Maybe this was the next step.

He bit his lip and stroked a single line of black ink on the page before him. There were things that actually mattered in the world, Inky knew, and just in case he forgot, his school served up heapings of world tragedy and disasters as part of the curriculum. But at this moment, the world, his world, depended on him drawing Amanda.

Principal Harooni's voice echoed in his head. *It's time.* He fixed on the crisp lettuce green. He knew the color he wanted. No other green would do. He took a deep breath.

Inky opened the door to his father's study. The shades were still drawn. The dust made him sneeze. He lowered his head as he walked to the desk. He didn't want to look around. He felt cold from the inside out. He squeezed his eyes tight, as if it would chase away the flood of images of his father working at his desk. He shivered from his shoulders all the way down his spine.

He bumped his knee against the wooden desk and felt for the drawer, pulled it open, grabbed the ink and raced out of the room. The sound of the door closing triggered a sea of color, emerald green swirling and turning darker, ever darker, into a menacing inky abyss.

He sat at his own desk for a long time until the shaking stopped. When his hand was steady again, he loaded the emerald green cartridge into his pen. He made a dot by his character's ear, added some water to dilute the color and then drew a circle, the spiral increasing slightly, over and over again. He repeated the same motion for the other earring.

At the top of the drawing he wrote *The Green Goddess* in letters that looked like a vine.

He scanned his drawing and signed on to the server handling the Megaland drop box. He attached his file with the message:

Picasso2B: I'm uploading another picture – I'm sure you'll find good use for it.

Chapter 17
The New, New Girl

WHEN AMANDA SIGNED ON TO MEGALAND, she was greeted by a silly animated graphic of wires touching that said "Testing in progress." She wondered about the other testers. What were they like? Did they live in New York? Would she ever get to meet them?

She opened her homework notebook and recalled some of the things that Hawk had said about their classmates. She wrote about a page and set it aside. The testing icon dissolved on the Megaland screen and the welcome screen came up. The chat box appeared.

Megaland: Welcome, welcome Justagirl. Sorry if I kept you waiting. I was just finishing up with the artist.

She felt her smile broaden. It was almost as if the website was hers alone. She wondered how long the development stage would be, and hoped it would be a long time.

Justagirl: Gave me time to do my home-work.

Megaland: That was quick. It must be easy for you.

Justagirl: Not really. The teacher is making me write about the school and I don't really know anyone so it's hard. And this time it matters, 'cause we're probably not moving again.

Megaland: I can see why you're worried. You want to make a good impression at your new school, but it must be hard to figure out how

Justagirl: Exactly.

Megaland: Used to be that if you were smart and pretty it all worked out. I know you're smart.

Justagirl: IDK.

Megaland: Well your work here has been fast and smart. Bet you're pretty, too.

Justagirl: Not really.

Megaland: Girls don't always realize how pretty they are to others. But never mind that. Why don't you take your mind off school and play a game? I have a new one. You inspired me. I'd really like to know what you think.

Justagirl: K.

A screen came up with instructions for a game based on visual puns. Amanda started reading.

"Some words are not what they seem – a traffic jam has nothing to do with fruit spread, and Dr. Pepper is not a chili with a medical degree. But what if you could take these words and illustrate them?"

When she reached the end of the screen, she clapped her hands in delight. This was just like what tripped her up in English. How thoughtful to create a game for her.

"Try this. Pick a word from the list. Then look at the graphics to find the pictures that match. With the edit tool you can resize the elements and add backgrounds and colors."

Amanda looked over the list: traffic jam, chick-in-soup, Dr. Pepper, brain wash, crow bar, grandfather clock.

She picked "brain wash." There were more images of brains to choose from than she expected. Not just gray science-y illustrations, but also cartoons, drawings and the one picture she chose—a jello mold in the shape of a brain. For "wash" she picked a brightly colored box of detergent. She played with the editing tool a bit to get the brain the right size to fit in the box. Her creation filled the screen.

Then a burst appeared saying, "You've earned points." The text box reappeared at the bottom of her screen.

Justagirl: That was fun. Silly. But fun.

Megaland: I need to think of more puns. Perhaps you can help me with that. Every time you hear a figure of speech, make a note of it and tell me.

Justagirl: K. now when girls at school say things like that, my confusion will be useful.

Megaland: You didn't click on the burst. Don't you want to see what's next?

Justagirl: Didn't know that was something to click on.

Megaland: Perfect. That's just the kind of feedback I need. Why don't you click on it now to see?

When Amanda clicked on the burst, the screen read: "You're one step closer to your dream date. Who will it be?"

Thumbnail images came up on the screen. They were pictures of guys, with the instruction "Click to enlarge."

She clicked on each one. There was a basketball player, a rocker, a slender guy with glasses and a briefcase and a big smile, and a guy in a suit with a confident smile and eyes that reminded her of her brother. She clicked on him.

A new screen came up. "Coming soon. Mix and Match, where you select the right shoes for your date outfit."

Then another screen came up. It was a picture of a stylish girl, sophisticated like a model, dressed in a purple jacket and gray pants. Her legs seemed to go on forever. The face looked familiar, though she couldn't place why. But it was the cool haircut that she kept looking at. It was asymmetrical and unlike anything Amanda had ever seen. She particularly liked how the part in the hair looked like a lightning bolt. How she would love to look like that.

Amanda was so absorbed in the image on the screen that she didn't hear her mother come in. From behind her, her mother gasped. Amanda was startled and screamed.

"Manda, what are you looking at? That's so you! Are you trying one of those makeover programs?"

"Mama, I didn't hear you come in."

"Oh, *mija*, I didn't mean to startle you. I love what you're looking at," her mother said. "Such a clever girl, you are. It's perfect, perfect."

Amanda looked at the cursor blinking in the chat box. She hit the keyboard.

Justagirl: GTG. POS.

As she typed "POS," she thought to herself that she'd never had any reason to type that before. So rarely was a parent over her shoulder, and rarer still that she had anything of her own, or had anything to hide.

"I was just playing around." Amanda didn't know why exactly, but she was relieved that her mother didn't ask any more about the game.

"You could look like that. I think you're right. Do you want a new look?"

Amanda nodded. She could imagine the Sacred Circle girls talking about that haircut.

"Print out that picture, Manda. Let's get you a keratin and a new haircut. I'll have daddy's secretary set it up for you and me. It's time for a New York look."

* * *

At first the mirrors in the hair salon made Amanda cringe. The hairstylist, whom Amanda dubbed Edwina Scissorhands for her spider black hair and leather pants, took one look at the printout of the Megaland haircut and said awesome so many times, Amanda lost count.

She liked being fussed over this way, and sometime between the shampoo and color and the blow dry, Amanda began to believe that with this haircut she was, as Edwina said, "Not just some ordinary girl. Somebody. You walk down the street with this cut and your long legs, and people'll think, 'There goes somebody.'"

Then while her mother was getting her hair cut, Amanda walked around Madison Avenue. She felt a little like she was in a costume and kept looking at strangers to see their reaction. She stopped in a store that had greeting cards, notebooks and desk supplies. She thought she might pick up something for her brothers—she wanted to give them something special this Christmas. Each time she turned an item over and saw the price tag, she put it back. Even if she saved every penny of her allowance, she wouldn't be able to afford much more than a paperweight in this store.

She caught her reflection in a window, fluffed her hair and twisted the little plum curl around her index finger and saw a girl who was no longer plain and spindly. She smiled and waved; it was like she was meeting someone new.

Chapter 18
Compare and Contrast

I T FELT LIKE THE SCHOOL HALLWAY contracted when the bell between classes rang. Inky tucked his chin to his chest and headed towards his science classroom. It was like swimming against the tide, a tide of soccer players led by Sven and his wingmen.

Just behind the Soccer Boys, Hawk, in a voice that sounded like wheels scraping on pavement, called out, "Halloween's coming, Artboy. Get on your inner spook."

The Soccer Boys from both classes laughed, saying, "Good one, Hawk" and "Truth."

Inky saw Amanda walking behind Hawk. She lowered her head and looked away. He thought she was embarrassed, but was it because of what Hawk had said or was she embarrassed to see him? Rungs, who was jammed in the center, shot Inky a sympathetic glance.

Inky wanted to say something to Hawk, but nothing came to mind. He glared at her, trying to pierce her with his gaze. It worked like a camera, and seared the moment into his memory.

"Look with intention and attention," his father would say when Inky was younger. Inky hadn't quite understood the words at the time, but he had still developed the technique. His inner spook.

Inky entered the class with the image of Hawk in the hallway emblazoned on his brain. Mr. Wallingford, the science teacher, touched the ends of his moustache and introduced the day's lesson.

"The scientific method," the teacher said with that reverence Inky's mother also used for the names of the miracle drugs her company manufactured. What was it about science anyway?

"For our purposes today, the scientific method is the process used to answer questions and explain phenomena outside the realm of coincidence."

Inky wrote this down as the teacher paused to allow the class to finish. He had the intention of taking notes on the four steps of the scientific method, which Mr. Wallingford promised they "would learn to abide and respect." Inky wrote *four steps* right under the definition in his boxy precise handwriting

"Step One: Observation and Description." Mr. Wallingford talked about the importance of noting all the details, even if they don't immediately seem important to you. "Think of something you've seen recently and describe it."

Hawk in the hallway was fresh in Inky's mind. As the class noted features of their chosen objects, Inky started drawing. He began with a strong, sharp line that arched into a birdlike body.

"The next step is the formulation of a hypothesis to explain the phenomena. This can be expressed as a simple statement, like 'objects fall down'; or a more complex equation, like 'when baking soda and vinegar are mixed, they erupt,'" the teacher said.

"Hawk is a dangerous creature." Inky wrote below his doodle. He continued drawing, adding talons and feathers to the chest.

The teacher circled the room. Inky felt Mr. Wallingford approaching and looked up from his paper, straight into his teacher's eyes as if in rapt attention. Then Inky went back to work. He drew an arrow through the breast of the bird, poking through an oversized heart, broken and bleeding.

"Step Three is to use your hypothesis to predict the results of new observations or other phenomena."

He wrote down the words "*Other phenomena. New observations.*" There was something nagging at him, just below his consciousness.

Inky's brain panned to Amanda, standing beside Hawk. He noted her little diamond stud and the length of her face, so familiar to him from drawing it. He mentally traced the line to the top of the forehead under the thick mane of hair.

"Step Four: properly performed experiments that can be duplicated by independent sources," the teacher said.

Inky went over the details. What was different? He only caught a glimpse of Amanda and he'd been focused on her eyes to read her expression. He tried to isolate the image, forget the hallway and the Soccer Boys and Hawk and her talons laced into Amanda. He focused on his mental image of Amanda: her face was tilted, her head was down, her hair was . . . smoother and definitely not in a ponytail.

"That's it," Inky said out loud as he realized that Amanda had cut her hair. His classmates tittered.

"That's right, Mr. Kahn. That's it. Four steps. Four elegant steps." Mr. Wallingford walked towards Inky's seat, his lanky frame casting a shadow on Inky's notebook.

"Would you like to share your hypothesis with the class?"

"I, er, I didn't think they were for sharing."

"I see. Yes," Mr. Wallingford said, glancing at Inky's notebook. "I see. This is not art class, and as much as I think there is an idea there, you must be able to clearly articulate your hypothesis. That is the scientific method. It must be clear for others to duplicate."

Mr. Wallingford returned to the front of the classroom. "I'll remind you all that along with the ability to compare and contrast, the scientific method is a core skill that you are required to master. I suggest you spend some time learning the steps."

Inky knew that shorthand. His head filled with a deep indigo. He was failing science.

With that the teacher handed them the results of their pop quizzes. On the right corner of his classmates' papers, Inky could see checkmarks. On his there was a big red "F."

On the way out the door, Mr. Wallingford called out to Inky, "You're welcome to see me for extra help, Mr. Kahn."

"Thanks," Inky called out, "but I gotta run today." Inky rushed down the hallway to the lockers. He wanted to get another look at Amanda.

Inky grabbed his books and headed toward Rungs's locker, which was near Amanda's. He looked over in their direction and saw Hawk take her skateboard out of her locker. He quickly looked away. A moment later, standing by Rungs's locker, he caught a glimpse of Amanda reaching into her locker. He had a full view of the back of her head. Inky could see her hair taper to reveal the back of her neck. As Amanda stood up, he saw a plum-colored strand of hair on her face.

He looked away, but not soon enough. He felt his checks burn. She'd seen him looking at her. He tried to change his expression from shock to a smile, but it was too late. She'd already turned to listen to whatever Hawk had to say.

Rungs caught him looking in the direction of Amanda and Hawk.

"Let it go, dude. Hawk's a case. Damaged goods," Rungs said.

"It's not that."

"Total malware."

Inky shook his head. "Right. Get me virus protection."

Inky looked back at Amanda one more time and caught a glimpse of the sharp edge of one side of her hair. It was like a current went through him. The part in her hair was jagged like a lightning bolt, just like he'd drawn.

* * *

At the Broken Cup coffee house, Inky weaved through the after-school crowd and grabbed a table while Rungs got a sweet tea for him and a double espresso for himself. He thumbed through his sketchbook and looked at his drawings for Megaland. The drawings definitely resembled

Amanda—just more grown up and sophisticated. And with a slammin' haircut.

Rungs put Inky's change on the table along with their drinks. They took off the lids of their drinks. While Rungs opened his third sugar, Inky asked, "Did you notice that Amanda's hair is different?"

"Huh?"

"Amanda. The new girl. In your classes."

"Yeah," Rungs said.

"'Yeah,' new haircut, or 'yeah,' you know who I mean?"

Rungs put his coffee down and stared at him. "I know who you mean. Yes, she looked different today."

"Last week Amanda had long, wild hair. Now she has a jagged part and bangs with plum highlights."

"Dude, you sound like a fashion magazine. You wanna talk about girls' haircuts?" Rungs sipped his coffee. "You *like* her."

"No."

"It's OK to like a girl."

"I don't know her really. She's the new girl." Inky looked down at his tea.

"There are advantages to new," Rungs said.

Like she doesn't know I'm the walking wounded. At least she didn't until Hawk got hold of her, Inky thought. "Even if I liked her, that's not the point."

"Dude, that's big." Rungs clapped his hand on Inky's shoulder.

"Will you listen to me? I don't want to talk about who likes who."

"No?"

Inky looked around the café and lowered his voice. "I drew her haircut, and then she got it cut."

"Say what?"

"Her haircut. It's a particular haircut."

"So?" Rungs said. "That's an American girl thing. They're always getting haircuts."

"But not *this* haircut. It's my haircut. From my drawing. And she's not American."

"Ooh. You've got it bad, dude."

"Negatory." Inky shook his head vigorously.

Rungs raised his eyebrows. "I detect a case of full-blown like."

Inky banged the table. He hated that he was so transparent, hated that he was such a ball of confusion. It was hard to know what you felt when you hadn't let yourself feel for so long. "Cut it out. She got the haircut just like my drawing. Why did she get that haircut?"

Rungs shrugged. "She liked how it looked?"

Inky rolled his eyes.

"If the art thing fails, you can be a hairdresser." Rungs held up his fingers like scissors.

Inky threw a sugar packet at Rungs and shook his head. "She had to have seen my sketchbook. But how? You know I never let it out of my sight."

"What about gym?" Rungs said, now taking Inky seriously. "Did you leave it in your gym locker for Sven and the barbarians to get hold of?"

"Possible. But last year when they messed with me, they signed the inside of my locker. They're not subtle."

"True that."

"She's hanging out with Hawk."

"There you go."

"Yeah, right." He flashed on the image of Hawk with talons from his drawing in science class. "I don't know."

Rungs finished off his coffee and put the cup down. "Dude, she got her hair cut, right? Probably saw it in a magazine. Didn't you say your mom was reading all these girl stuff magazines? You probably drew a haircut you saw in one of them."

"I dunno. Maybe. But I really thought it was unique." Inky weighed the possibility that Rungs was right. He felt relieved that it might be a coincidence, but crestfallen that his drawing and ideas might not be as original as he'd thought.

"That's gotta be it if no one saw your sketches," Rungs said. "You didn't upload them to the school server or anything?"

"After you hacked it last year? I totally know better." But as Inky said that he had a flicker of memory. He thought of his father's study and the green ink and scanning his drawings for Megaland. "I did upload it for Megaland—you know, that game developer you turned me on to."

Rungs put down his coffee and focused on Inky. "How'd you send it?"

"It was too big for email. The guy had me upload it to one of those drop box sites."

It was as if a computer had come out of hibernate mode; Inky could practically hear Rungs calculating possibilities. "They're usually pretty secure. Did you title it? Any words or tags? Anything that'd be picked up in search?"

"Nah."

Rungs waved his hand dismissively. "It's a magazine. Ask her where she got the idea for her haircut. Girls like that kind of thing." He winked at Inky.

"When did you become such an expert on girls?"

Rungs laughed. "I've found mine, so I've got plenty of time to observe."

"I guess you're right," Inky said, but he really didn't think so. He felt like something was amiss— had felt that way ever since he drew the Green Goddess picture. He felt an uncomfortable fullness in his chest and throat. A swirl of dark color filled his head.

"Dude, you're not looking so good. You feel OK?"

"I feel—I guess, it's just, I dunno. You're probably right and all, but something's creepy." The dark colors receded as he said that. Rungs's calm silence invited him to say more.

"Maybe it's just that I went into my father's study." It was a lot to share, and he felt embarrassed, naked.

Rungs was good. He looked at Inky intently for a moment. "His spirit," he said quietly. Inky nodded. Rungs made a funny gesture with his hands, shaking them over the table. "*Pii,*" Rungs said.

The word had a high-pitched tone that startled Inky and made him suck in his breath. "*Pii,*" Rungs said again, softly, almost reverently. "In your father's study, spirits."

"Spirits?" he asked, looking at Rungs.

"Your dad's spirit. Wandering around. It's because you don't have a spirit house. The spirits of the dead need someplace to go."

Inky nodded and let out his breath. He knew Rungs took his customs and religion seriously, but he was annoyed anyway. For a year and a half, everyone told him what to do and feel and what he was doing wrong. He'd always been grateful that Rungs had kept from judging him. Until now.

Inky glared at Rungs, but the look didn't stop him.

"You're feeling uneasy because your dad's spirit is wandering and looking for you."

In his own way Rungs was saying the same thing as the Soccer Boys in the cafeteria and Hawk in the hallway. Inky was like a haunted house. How stupid of him to think that his friend didn't think so, too. And Amanda? If she didn't connect the dots herself, Hawk by now must have clued her in.

"I'm six feet tall, dude. I shouldn't be so hard to find," Inky said.

"You're hiding from the spirit. Hiding what matters. What you care about. Even who you care about."

That's enough, Inky thought and banged the table. Because I didn't want to tell him about a crush I maybe have, he hits me with this mystic dung.

"You're hiding from them—and yourself," Rungs added.

"Thank you, cosmic muffin," Inky said, feeling hot from the anger rising inside of him. "And thanks for the lesson on ghosts. I'll be sure to make a little house for the spirits. Maybe I'll use a cardboard box like we did in fourth grade."

Rungs picked up his coffee cup and slowly crushed it. "Open up, will you. I was just trying to help you get a little peace."

Chapter 19
Inky Cleans Up

INKY CAME HOME TO AN EMPTY APARTMENT. The familiar creak of the old floorboards reminded him of Rungs's talk about spirits. He winced. He regretted that he'd been so nasty to Rungs, but why'd he have to say all that stuff?

As he walked to the back of the apartment, his head filled with murky colors; they swirled, like a squid's ink, marking everything. Inky tried to shake it off, but with the darkness came a deep cold. He felt pulled to his father's study. He pictured it, shades drawn, papers strewn about, and could practically smell the must of disuse.

Whether or not he believed what Rungs said about ghosts and spirits, his father had never let his study get dusty and wouldn't be happy with what it looked like now. The least he could do, then, was to do what he knew was right.

He found the cleaning bucket with the dust rags and cleansers under the bathroom sink and entered his father's study. It felt like night because of the blackout shade. Inky released it. The shade's thwack echoed in the empty room as it rolled up, setting off a dance of dust in the stream of late afternoon sun.

Outside the window Inky saw the maple tree shedding its copper and rust-hued leaves. He'd forgotten how he'd loved to sit on the mushroom-colored beanbag chair under the window. He dragged it from the other side of the room and whacked it. The dust made him cough, but he whacked it a few more times because it felt good.

There were still papers from his father's last trip strewn across the desk. His father had pulled the project together in a hurry, and this time, of course, there'd been no post-trip tidying. Inky looked at the appointment card from the tropical disease specialist who'd given Inky's dad the shots and medicine before the trip. The date looked like ancient history. He wished he could go back to that day, or to any day before it.

Deeper into the pile of papers, Inky recognized the Brazilian postmark and name of his father's friend who'd set up the trip. He opened one of the letters and immediately felt guilty for snooping. Then he realized it didn't matter, and read about the Indian tribe, how his father's friend Raoul had first found them because of a stray headband that was decorated in a pattern he'd not seen used by other known indigenous tribes.

Inky put the letter back in the envelope. He gathered the other cards and papers, then stacked them, tied them with rubber bands and put them in the biscotti tin where his father kept his password notebook and other business papers. Then he put cleanser on some paper towels and scrubbed the newly revealed desk surface.

Inky moved over to the bookcase and blew the dust off of the books. He touched the leaves of a dead plant and threw it out. He flipped through the huge pile of old *Traveler* and *National Geographic* magazines. He took a few things to read and placed the rest in a bag to give to the school librarian.

Inky took his rag and wiped down the windowsill, the blinds and the edges of the bookshelves. He took care to clean out all the crannies of a carved wooden mask. When he was done, he patted it on its head. Then he swept.

As he was emptying the dustpan, Inky heard his mother open the apartment door. He stopped, knowing she'd see the sliver of sunlight coming from his father's study when she walked through the entranceway.

"What are you doing? Who said you could go in there?" his mother shouted before even saying hello.

"I'm cleaning."

Her tone reflected her shock, Inky knew, but he was pissed she didn't acknowledge he was doing something good, something hard.

She looked from the magazines in the bag to the discarded plant in the trash. She crossed her arms across her chest. "Michael Kahn."

"It needed to be done. It may not bother you because you're never around."

She uncrossed her hands and put them on her hips. "What have you done?"

His anger at his mother mingled with his raw feelings from his afternoon with Rungs, and he lashed out. "You think it's time to start dating, Ma. I think it's time to clean up, OK. What do you think Dad would prefer?"

His mother gasped. "Mikey."

"And don't call me Mikey." Inky turned his back on her, ripped off a sheet of paper towel, sprayed it with glass cleaner and wiped the glass of the photograph on his father's desk. It was a picture of the three of them on the beach at Montauk the summer after fourth grade. Just behind their heads was a sign: "No lifeguard on duty. Swim at your own risk." Ain't that the truth, he thought.

Inky felt his mother's gaze looking at the photograph, too. "It's just. This is so unexpected; I had no warning, I . . ." Her voice was softer.

"I cleaned up. The dust and clutter won't bring him back."

"Michael Kahn."

"What?" Inky said, crossing the room to look out at the tree. "Why are you mad?"

She slapped her thigh for emphasis. "It's not yours to decide that today is the day to throw out his stuff. Didn't you think I'd want to be part of that decision?" Her face contorted. "No, of course not. It was like that when he was alive. You and your dad, it was like a boys' club. Doing whatever you pleased."

Her words pierced him. He'd wished she'd slapped him instead of making him feel like he had to defend his father. "That's because you were never around. You're married to your work."

His mother started sobbing. He'd never seen her like this, though sometimes he'd heard her cry at night when she thought he was asleep. He just stared.

"Did you ever think that I need you? That you're all I have left of him?" his mother said after a minute.

She walked towards him then stopped. Inky thought he saw her hands come up from her sides, and was half-expecting a hug from her, like when he was little and hurt. But she didn't come closer.

"You sure have a funny way of showing it. It's not like you've exactly been there for me, you know."

"You don't know how hard I tried."

"Oh yeah, you tried," Inky said.

"I tried not making any demands on you—errands around the house, forget that. Not going to school. I covered for you. The school psychologist, even grief counseling—which I understand was a big help for your classmate, Helen, when she lost her mother."

"Yeah, Ma, Hawk's real together now."

"I don't care about her, Michael, I care about you."

"You care about me. Great. What I cared about? It's gone. All gone. Besides Dad, all I ever wanted was to go to Art & Design. Dad said I could transfer out of MDA for high school. And what, Ma, what? I screwed up so bad I couldn't even apply. And you just stood by and watched while I failed."

Inky bit his lip hard. He wasn't going to cry.

"You shut yourself down and locked me out. Locked everything out. There was no reaching you to help," his mother said.

He wanted to be mad, but he recognized the truth in what she said, a truth that was echoed by Rungs earlier in the day.

Inky looked up at the carved wooden mask and his father's things. Some of the anger inside was replaced by understanding; it was almost like he was seeing his mother and himself in a mirror.

"It started when they hung the mural at school. He would have been so proud, but he wasn't there. Every time something happened and he wasn't there to see it, it was like he died all over again. So I shut down. It didn't seem fair that life could go on just like always. To go on made it seem like he never mattered."

"Oh, Inky." She put her arms around him. It was stiff, but it helped. Somehow he believed she was doing the best that she could.

After a moment she cleared her throat and returned to her more remote self.

"Thank you for cleaning up. You're right. He would have wanted this. But shouldn't you be spending time on your schoolwork?

"Schoolwork? We're talking about schoolwork?"

"Well, dear, Principal Harooni called today to say there was a watch on your file."

"A watch. Does it tell time? Oops, sorry. Lame joke. But really, what do they expect? It's the first month of school."

"It's time to turn the corner. You know the consequences if you fail your core subjects."

"I'm making good progress on my presentation. So far, Mrs. Patel really likes my drawings."

Inky's mother raised an eyebrow. "Perhaps you can talk to your teachers then and find out what they want from you."

As she walked out, she gave him another stiff hug meant to make him feel better. It did not.

His legs felt like jelly, and he sunk into the beanbag chair. He was deeply tired; the day's events swirled in primary colors in his head like a spin art: Amanda's haircut, his big red "F" for epic fail on the science quiz, the fights with his mother and Rungs. It was like a centrifugal force was drawing it all outward, lifting it away from him, creating an intricate, layered image.

He glanced up at the bookshelves. The mask seemed to smile down on him. The study felt calm. The spirits, at least, were at peace.

* * *

Later in his room, he sent an IM to Rungs.

Inky: You have spirit houses. We have Fantastik and Windex. Sorry I blew up. U were right.

Chapter 20
If the Shoe Fits

AMANDA WHISTLED AS SHE THREW her books down on the bed. With Hawk helping her, she didn't dread her project so much.

She looked into the mirror and put her hands on her hips in exaggerated toughness, mimicking Hawk. Then she put one hand up and rested her head on it, like a model's pose. She looked "fierce," to borrow a Hawk word.

Amanda turned on her music. She felt like dancing. The song sounded better coming from her computer than the last time she'd heard it, on a tinny player in the Nairobi market. She saw that there was an email from her brother Derek.

He told her how hard his classes were and how there were more people in his own dorm than in their last two schools combined. He'd even run into the son of the ambassador from Benin. Did she remember, he asked, that they'd lived in the same area in France when Amanda was really young? At the end he said he missed her, wondered how she was adjusting to her new school and asked if their parents were spoiling their baby girl rotten.

Amanda wrote that she was becoming a New York sophisticate. "You may not recognize your baby sister when you see me again." She didn't let herself miss him.

She opened her project notes and jotted down some of what Hawk had told her about the different friendship groups at the school. She giggled as she remembered Hawk telling her about the time prissy Priya planned the group outing to Serendipity then barfed frozen hot chocolate on Sven Thorsson's shoes.

The Sacred Circle shopped together, and it showed. When they had something new, like the brown burlap "Feed" bag that they all used as a book bag, others in the school, Amanda now included, soon followed. Amanda made a note of the irony. Here they were in a school that celebrated diversity, and all they all wanted was to fit in.

It was a good point, but there was nothing special to the rest of what she wrote. She'd have to work on weaving in Hawk's stories. She saved her work and played a couple of rounds of word scramble. When she didn't see that "nekstit" was "kittens," she gave up and signed on to Megaland.

Megaland: Hello again, Justagirl. How are you liking autumn in New York?

Justagirl: The colors are pretty.

Megaland: It's my favorite season – harvest time. Time to enjoy all the fruits of your labor. My work is progressing. I would welcome your feedback on the next elements.

Justagirl: The dressing up game?

Megaland: Yes, that's it. You have a wonderful memory.

Justagirl: I was looking forward to it. I started to pay more attention to what everyone is wearing.

Megaland: I'll be most interested in what you think.

The chat box minimized and the screen was filled by a giant closet. A model stepped to the front. Amanda recognized her—she'd inspired Amanda's transformation. Now she was in a black derby, a double-breasted satin jacket and jeans. Her toes wiggled, which made Amanda laugh.

The model pointed to the shoe rack in the closet. Amanda clicked on a pair of black patent pumps. The model's head shook no. Amanda scanned the shoe rack and selected a pair of bronze booties. The model clapped and retreated to the closet. She returned in a flowered mini with a touch of lace at the hem. Amanda recognized this as the kind of thing Priya or Ellen would wear over black leggings. She knew what shoes they'd wear, and immediately clicked on the black ballet flats. The shoes moved from the rack and rested to the side of the model. But there was no applause.

For a second Amanda was unsure what to do. The model's toes wiggled.

Amanda spotted a pair of black leather boots at the back of the closet. They were thigh-highs. When she clicked on them they moved to the front of the closet and sat on top of a pile of shoeboxes. She wasn't sure what do, so she clicked on the box labeled size 8, her size. She thought she'd clicked on the wrong thing again, but the model applauded. The ballet flats returned to the rack and then disappeared off screen. A gift box appeared on the closet floor. Amanda waited for the model to return to open it. The text box enlarged.

Megaland: Did you like that?

Justagirl: It was fun. I'm still learning about fashion.

Megaland: Would you like to have a closet like that and dress up?

Justagirl: Totally. That would be cool.

Megaland: Did you notice the gift on the closet floor? You missed the reward file once before. Maybe the placement is wrong. Or maybe the timing? What do you think?

Justagirl: I think it's ok. I'll open it now. It's just that after I play, it's fun to chat. I like that my opinion matters.

Megaland: Oh it does. Your feedback will make this more successful. In fact it's time to move you into a higher testing level.

Justagirl: wow.

Megaland: If I were able to pay for user testing, what would you buy with the money you'd earn?

Justagirl: IDK

Megaland: Clothes? Shoes? Girls like shoes. Or makeup? Or how about those boots?

Justagirl: The boots are fierce. But I'm saving to buy holiday presents.

Megaland: We're gearing up for a round of on-site user testing. We need to do it soon. I'll let you know as soon as we can arrange it.

Justagirl: cool

Amanda clicked on the gift box that appeared on screen. The gift card said: "*Well done. You've made it to another level. You'll look like a goddess on your dream date.*"

This feels a little young, Amanda thought. But it was kind of fun to think about dating.

A model emerged from the box. As it resolved, Amanda leaned in to the screen. The image was amazing—a beautiful girl dressed in a dark and light green gown. The skirt part looked like billowy triangles. Handkerchief style, Amanda thought it was called. She was meant to be a princess, or a goddess; there was a crown of leaves around the model's forehead and a flower of broccoli in her hair.

She looked again. The dress was totally unique. There was an unusual texture to the fabric.

It had to be. She looked again. This was not a standard fairy tale princess. The dress, as she looked closer, was definitely made from lettuce leaves. What she first took for pearl earrings she now saw were peas.

A vegetable princess. She gasped. The goddess of salad! She thought of Inky right away. Hadn't he said he always loved to draw? And that first day, he wouldn't let his friend Rungs write on a page from his sketchbook. She could see why. His work was amazing.

No one had ever done anything like this for her. No one had paid that much attention to her. She was not sure what to make of it, but she was definitely enticed by the thoughtful, complex boy behind this game.

The cursor blinked. She'd been ignoring the text box while she took the image in.

Megaland: Do you like it?

Megaland: Is it too odd? Too green? Tell me what you think.

Justagirl: I love it. It's perfect. My very own Green Goddess.

Chapter 21
Conjecture and Proof

INKY HADN'T SEEN HER COMING. The conversation lasted for only a moment, but he shuddered from the impact. Amanda, with a shy-girl flush on her cheeks, walked up to his table at the cafeteria, held up a piece of broccoli from her plate and said, "I'll wear this on my date, along with green pea earrings. Like a Green Goddess." Then she smiled and walked away.

Inky watched her walk to the center of the cafeteria, his mouth open in disbelief. It was all so deliberate, so awkward, so rehearsed.

He looked at Rungs. "WTF?"

"WTG," Rungs said slowly, pronouncing each letter. "I think she just asked you out. Way to go."

"I don't believe it."

"Heard it with my own ears. She broke free from her buddy, Hawk, and as good as asked you out."

"That's not it," Inky said.

"I heard her say date."

"She did not say anything about a date with me," Inky said to Rungs. "And it's the other stuff that was *really* weird."

"That she's planning her outfit?"

"I don't know a lot about fashion, but I'm pretty sure that wearing vegetables is not a thing this year. There is no magazine that's showing that." Inky banged the table. "The green pea earrings, the broccoli flower. She got that from one of my drawings."

"For real?"

"Absolutely. Look."

Inky opened his notebook, thumbing through the pages so quickly he almost tore one. He stopped at some of the sketches he'd done for the Green Goddess drawing the previous week. Rungs stared at it for awhile.

"OTH, dude, this is off the hook good. But the vegetable dress thing. What's that about? The core project or something?"

"Or something," Inky said. "Someone, like Hawk, must've got hold of my drawing and shown Amanda. The question is how."

"Ask Amanda."

Inky shook his head no. "It's probably some trap. Hawk put her up to it. And I'm not falling for it."

"She seems to like you. Ask her."

"I can't," Inky said, lowering his head so his chin was almost to his chest. Talking to girls, being with girls, talking with anyone, in fact, that was normal stuff. But not for him. The grief he felt had turned him to stone. He hated it, but accepted it. That was the way it was now. "I just can't ask her, all right?"

Rungs was quiet for a moment, then asked, "So how do you think she got the picture?"

"I don't know. I don't do that kind of thing. I never even cheated on a math test. But I know that the only time I don't have my sketchbook is gym."

"If Hawk cut gym, she coulda gotten into your locker and copied the picture for Amanda."

Inky nodded.

"But," Rungs said, "why would she bother?"

"Hawk never forgave me for the cartoon I did of her in middle school. She was all into riding horses out in the Hamptons. I drew her like Lady Godiva, but with a crown and a whip. In a bank vault. It didn't have her name on it, but everyone knew it was her."

"That's ancient history. Plus, word was you made her look hot. It's gotta be something more than that," Rungs said.

True. There was always more with Hawk.

He had known her forever, when she was still called Helen, before she practically swapped her feet for a skateboard and renamed herself in honor of her skateboard hero. Hawk, the daughter of a prominent international banker, the center of the popular group, always seemed to have everything.

But Hawk had turned to him for the one thing she ever needed, and he'd turned her away.

Her mother died a couple of months after his father's accident. Hawk was making Inky pay for his coldness to her, even in the grief therapy group, was making everyone pay for her grief. But he had nothing to give, had no wisdom or understanding or coping strategies. She'd had plenty of time to be prepared during the two years her mother was sick. His father's death was sudden and haunted him still. No, he had nothing for her, and now, he was sure, she was making him pay for his weakness.

"Hawk has reason enough," Inky said.

"It's just conjecture, dude. You need proof," Rungs said.

"You sound like Wallingford," Inky said of the science teacher.

"Nah—it'll take Wallingford another month to get to conjecture and proof at the rate he's teaching."

"Unless . . ." said Inky. He stopped himself, considering his words. "I don't see how it's possible, but . . ."

"What?" Rungs asked.

"I sent that picture to Woody, the Megaland dude, for the game. But I don't even know if he used it. I can't imagine how she'd get a hold of it. "

Rungs was looking down at his minicomputer, which he held under the table, careful to hide it because of the "no devices in the school building" rule.

"Are you with me?" Inky said.

"Yup. Checking the student directory for Amanda's address."

"What do you need that for?" Inky asked.

"You want to see if she got the picture from the game developer? We need to know where she lives. Or at least where her computer lives." He looked back down. "NG. No go on the address or phone number. Just her email. C'mon. Let's go make a phone call."

Inky and Rungs went outside to the MDA parking lot. A group of senior girls sat against the back wall, texting in unison. Inky could tell from their expressions when they were texting each other.

Rungs punched in a phone number. "*Sa wha dee kharap*," he said into the phone. To Inky it sounded like Rungs said 'so what the crap,' an odd greeting, and oddly appropriate. He giggled a nervous giggle. An Indonesian boy smoked a clove cigarette. Inky moved so that he was out of his wind but still within earshot of Rungs, who was speaking in Thai.

He smiled and nodded. "*Khob khun na kharap*," he said. "Thank you so much."

"Who'd you call?" Inky asked when Rungs hung up.

"My father's secretary. Told her I went to school with the daughter of the Director of the World Assistance Agency and I promised I'd help her with her math homework—but I lost her address and phone number and I didn't want her to think that I'm dumb."

Inky let out a whistle. "If it doesn't work out with Apsara, you're going to be some player."

"Whatever," Rungs said, texting Amanda's information to Inky. "We'll check this out later."

* * *

Inky and Rungs hustled across the intersection right before the light changed, practically running into the plaza adjacent to the sky-hued glass building bearing Amanda's address. As he caught his breath, Inky recalled an abstract he'd done during the building's construction, depicting the angular line of a crane hoisting the big blue window panes over the forest green scaffolding. The way the sun hit the finished building made him think about toning down the blue he'd used for the glass.

"Perfect," said Rungs, who'd installed himself on a bench and immediately started typing stuff into his device. His expression was serious, but Inky caught a sparkle in his eye as he scanned a list on his screen. Inky tried to shake off the sci fi feeling as his mind bounced from his recollection of his painting to the building before him.

Rungs scrolled through the list of accessible wireless connections, creating 10-second novels about their owners. Inky thought that he'd never seen his friend so happy.

"Catinthehat, the password must rhyme. Popsicletoes wears some sweet kicks. OB123, they deliver. 12B, Netgear77. EinBear, hide your honey. Here we go. `Director`. I'm betting on director. Her dad's mighty proud of his position."

"Aren't those connections all secure?" Inky asked.

"No worries. Most routers have a quick setup that says to enter a password the whole family can remember. You'd be surprised how many people use a phone number. Which you happen to have."

Inky read the numbers off of Rungs's text.

"Most people don't read the part about creating a strong password. No one reads manuals."

Inky saw the icon for a successful connection appear on Rungs's toolbar. "Except you," he said. "You got into her computer?" Inky asked.

"That's just step one," Rungs said. "Tonight I'll send her a trojan."

"Say what? Gross."

"Not that kind of Trojan. It's like bugging a phone instead of listening at the door. You send a file that'll attach to the other person's computer— you've seen those spam messages that have something you're supposed to click on."

"You know how to do that?" Inky asked with a mix of awe and suspicion.

"I've never had a reason to try it," Rungs said.

Inky could tell his friend was happy to have that chance now.

A tree in the plaza outside Amanda's building cast a long shadow. The sun was beginning to go down. They waited for Amanda to sign on. Inky did his Spanish homework, then his math homework. He honestly felt like going home and working on his core presentation. Or just going home. He longed to be in his room or any place that was warm. But he couldn't complain. Rungs was doing this for him.

Chapter 22
Justagirl in Trouble

IT WAS THE SECOND AFTERNOON OF WAITING. Waiting, Inky noted, made him both bored and tense at the same time. He now knew more about SMTP and network protocols than he figured he'd ever need. To pass the time, Inky drew a mental picture of the encryption technique Rungs was explaining; onion routing with layers of secrecy would make a fine new abstract. Rungs continued with his mini-course in electronic espionage, describing how he'd built a RAT, a remote access Trojan, into a memo about a new rubric for the core project and sent it to Amanda. Inky pictured the beady eyes of a rubric rat, while Rungs explained how they'd now be able to see all of Amanda's computer activities.

But still there was the drudgery of waiting. At least they were using one of Rungs's modified tablets. The 10-inch screen seemed gigantic compared to the handheld they'd been using the first day.

"There's got to be a better way. We could wait here forever. We don't know when she logs on to her computer or the game. It could be late at night. What if her parents don't let her on the Internet until she's done with homework or something?"

They waited some more. Inky zipped the worn caramel-brown bomber jacket that had been his father's. He looked at the places the leather had cracked and thought of the barely paved road they'd traveled in Brazil. He wished everything didn't remind him of the accident. He wished he wasn't so haunted.

"Here we go," Rungs said, breaking the silence. It was getting dark, and even though Rungs had changed the type color on the screen to an electric orange against a black background, it was still hard to look at.

Inky could just make out a series of numbers and symbols. It looked like the gibberish he'd see when an email message bounced. Then he saw the familiar type and the Megaland welcome screen. He smiled in spite of himself.

"Whoa," Inky said louder than he'd wanted. "WTF. That's the game. That's Megaland. Amanda just signed on to Megaland."

"Keep it down," Rungs hissed, pointing to the skaters at the far end of the plaza.

Inky fixed his eyes on the screen. It seemed like there was some activity at the bottom of the screen.

He saw a string of numbers and letters where the chat box would normally open up.

"Dang," said Rungs, who started typing furiously. Something that looked like Cyrillic came on screen. The box faded. Rungs typed some more. Inky noticed his friend was sweating, despite the cool fall air.

Inky didn't quite understand what was happening with the computer but he was anxious to have it resolved. Now that they'd seen Amanda sign on to Megaland, he wanted to know what was going on.

"Gimme a minute," Rungs said, sensing Inky's tension.

Inky looked over at the skateboarders in the park. Maybe this had nothing to do with Hawk.

"Got it," Rungs said, his upper lip curled in self-satisfaction. A maze appeared and Inky and Rungs could see how Amanda's cursor sent a shiny black purse through the maze.

"Go left," Rungs said, giving instructions even though she couldn't possibly hear.

"You like this?" Inky asked. The purse jerked forward, flashing a bit of hardware as it got closer to the finish line. It was a weird feeling, like looking over someone's shoulder at an arcade.

Rungs shrugged. "Solving things works for me."

When the pocketbook made it through the maze, a giant gift box appeared on screen. Inky saw the arrow of Amanda's mouse.

Megaland: Click on the box this time.

Inky felt sick to see the familiar chat box—like a friend had found someone new to hang out with. The "this time" bothered him most.

All the other images faded, leaving the giant gift box. Its top came off in an animation sequence that was better than he would have expected. Virtual hot pink wrapping paper filled the screen. Then the box dissolved and a new scene appeared.

It was a party scene, a collage like a celebrity page in one of Inky's mom's magazines. The couple at the center of the scene didn't quite fit together, and the perspective was off. Inky felt smug—his work for the game was technically better than this, and more unique, too.

A flat-topped hat filled the top corner of the screen. Rungs saw it first.

"OMG," Rungs said.

There in red plaid and skinny jeans was Inky's hipster dude. Inky gasped. He'd been placed in the scene with the Amanda-like Megaland girl he'd first drawn, except that someone had retouched her outfit. Inky wondered if Woody had done it himself.

"No mistaking. That's your work," Rungs said. "Bingo. Mystery solved."

Suddenly Inky didn't want to see more. Even though he'd wanted to have his work used for a computer game, he didn't feel happy like he thought he would. Seeing it under these circumstances made it feel wrong.

"Wait," Rungs said, pointing to the corner of his screen. He put his arm out to keep Inky from getting up. "Check this out. They're chatting."

Inky moved closer, uncomfortably close to Rungs, in order to read the screen.

Justagirl: Ooh. I love eggnog.

Inky wondered how well they knew each other. Had they had as many conversations as he'd had with Woody? Was Amanda more a part of the game than he was?

Megaland: The holidays will be here sooner than you think.

"Doesn't it creep you out, spying on them?" Inky asked.

"Nah. You should hear the things my dad gets on tape sometimes. You wouldn't believe the things people say to each other." Rungs poked Inky to turn his attention back to the computer screen.

Justagirl: Don't remind me. I'm nowhere on presents for my brothers.

He nudged Rungs. "Do her brothers go to MDA?" Rungs shrugged.

Megaland: What do you want to give them?

Justagirl: Something that'll remind them of me.

"Sounds like they're not around," Inky said.

Megaland: Like a picture.

"What's 'like a picture?' A stick figure? " Rungs said.

Justagirl: That's brilliant.

Megaland: You said you liked your new haircut.

"Holy crap," Inky said.

Justagirl: A photograph of the new me. That's it. That's genius. You're a real pal, you know.

Megaland: Thank you. That means a lot to me. You have no idea how much.

Megaland: You know I have access to a studio. I can help you with your presents. We'll take pictures for your brothers for Christmas. Would that be a good gift? They'll see how much their baby sister has grown up.

Justagirl: Your artwork is so amazing. Makes sense you do photography. Bet you take great pictures, too.

Chapter 23
The Lines are Drawn

"I DON'T BELIEVE THIS," Inky said, kicking at the leaves on the sidewalk.

"Gotta admit your drawing looked great all animated like that. You gotta get yourself into a hipper art program. You should do that stuff," Rungs said.

Inky pictured a witch's cauldron, stinky and steaming. He thought he might be physically sick from all the feelings simmering inside of him. He remembered the instructions from the grief therapy group: *Breathe, first through your nose, then more deeply.* Right after her mother died, Hawk had suffered from panic attacks, so the whole group learned some coping skills. Turned out she was handy after all.

Rungs was talking faster and louder than Inky had ever heard him talk, like something let loose. Inky couldn't focus on the content. He kept seeing the orange type on the black screen and the words "your artwork is so amazing." "That's genius. You're

a real pal." The words echoed in his head. He'd
wished Amanda had said that to him. Who knew
what other conversations she'd had with Woody on
Megaland? Inky found the guy likeable enough;
why shouldn't she? He probably had great stories
to tell about rock stars he'd met when he was in the
music business. How could he compete with that?

On the other hand, Amanda did like his drawings, and that was something. Wasn't his art the
truest part of him? But then, did that mean she
thought she was talking to him when she was chatting with Woody? A him that was not him.

He banged his palm on his forehead and tried to
tune in to what Rungs was saying. ". . . something
we need to investigate, to find out more."

He did want to find out more about Amanda. He
didn't know much; just that he liked what she'd
said in assembly about being a citizen of the world,
liked how her face flushed and showed her shyness, liked that she was looking at him with fresh
eyes. Then the emotions bubbled up again, and in
Inky's head the cauldron steam turned into hot orange faces with frightful, toothy sneers.

He'd best not think anymore about Amanda.
Why should he care? He'd only get hurt. And he'd
been hurt enough already.

As they turned down Lexington Avenue towards
his building, Rungs was talking about Internet connections. Inky didn't quite get what Rungs was say-

ing. He was trying to concentrate, but it was like watching a video on the computer in the library—a little action, then a pause, buffering, buffering.

"We all leave digital fingerprints whether we know it or not," Rungs said in what sounded like a conclusion.

Inky had an image of hands with computer keys, mice and flash drives for digits, but the image got stuck. His mental sketchpad was on overload.

"Wait a minute," he said to Rungs. "Slow down. I missed something. I'm still freaked."

As they walked past the neighborhood playground, Rungs tapped Inky's shoulder and looked him in the eye. "We gotta find out who this guy is and why he wants to take Amanda's picture."

"You make it sound like a conspiracy or something," Inky said.

"Why would he take her picture? Why would he want to help her make gifts for her brothers? Did you ever think of that?" Rungs said.

"Because they're friends?" Inky said. "As far as she's concerned, they're schoolmates." He felt strange saying that; it was a little like when the adults in a room talk about you like you weren't there. "After all, who made her a Green Goddess?"

Rungs rolled his eyes. "That's her side of it. But what about him?"

Inky had to admit that he was too busy thinking about Amanda and how he felt about her to consider Woody's intentions. It wasn't something he really wanted to think about. He had so much else to turn over in his mind.

Not Rungs. He was calculating the possibilities, and clearly enjoying the challenge.

"Here's what we're going to do. We'll go back to your place—my dad's traveling anyway. You log on and talk to the game dude, and while you're online, I'll trace his IP address and check him out."

"You can come over, but talk to him?" he said to Rungs, "What can I say to him? 'I knew you'd use my stuff, but not this way. Not with a girl from my school.' What are the odds of that? Of it being Amanda?" Inky stopped for a second. It felt funny saying her name out loud. Funny in a good way.

"It's so frickin' weird," Inky continued. "What do I say to him? 'Don't give my drawings to any more girls? They're mine, give them back? Give him back.'"

Inky heard himself say "give him back." It had just slipped out. Rungs heard it, too.

"Give them back, I meant. Give them back." He was shaking. He knew this was all about more than just the game.

They walked silently for half a block. "You got me into this," Inky said to Rungs, breaking the awkwardness.

"Hey, I thought, you know, someone could see your drawings, maybe it would lead to something—get your mind off your dad."

Inky thought back to when Rungs first told him about the game. He replayed it frame by frame in his mind. "That's it. That's how it happened. The first day of school. She was sitting behind us. We didn't know her then, she was the new girl. Her notebook . . . you grabbed her notebook and wrote down the URL and access code."

"The ink must've gone through," Rungs said. "That's how she found out about the game. So of course she thinks it's you."

Inky didn't know if he should bless or curse his father's leaky pen.

* * *

There was no way for them to sit side by side in front of the computer in his room; still, Inky hesitated before leading Rungs to his father's study. As he opened the door, he felt like he was sharing a dark secret; it was scary, but it felt good. "We've gotta be done before my mom gets home," Inky said. He didn't want to give her a new reason to explode.

Inky sat at the big old wooden desk. Rungs plunked down on the beanbag chair under the window and fired up his computer. Inky turned on his father's machine.

He gasped at the screensaver: a picture of himself when he'd just turned 12. His hair was sun-bleached, in a classic long shag. There was a gleam of happiness in his eyes. In the background he could see the Wonder Wheel in Coney Island. He remembered the afternoon. On a lark he and his father took the subway, screamed and screamed on the roller coaster, then walked to the Russian shops in Brighton Beach to buy babka and smoked fish. So much had changed in two years.

"You need help with that?" Rungs asked.

"I can guess the password." He typed in "Picasso2B" and smiled as the computer connected. He missed being so special to someone.

"Can you get your email?" Rungs asked. "I just sent you something I want you to install. Click on the file and it'll let me see and capture your session."

While Inky installed the program and restarted the computer, Rungs explained, "Your IP, Internet Protocol, is like a street address for your computer. Every computer online has one. It's used to route information. It's a string of numbers. Too bad we don't have his email address—that would make it easier. Once we have his IP info, I'll try some tracing moves to see if we can get his info."

Inky took a deep breath and signed on to Megaland. The welcome screen looked different on his father's color-calibrated monitor. It took a few moments for the chat box to appear.

"He's got a sign-on notification. Chat box always come up like that?" Rungs asked.

"Yup." Inky nodded. "Figure it's because he's still building it."

"That's not gonna last past beta," Rungs said.

Megaland: Welcome back, Picasso2B. What brings you to Megaland today?

Picasso2B: DK. bored I guess. How's it going?

Megaland: The beta testing is going well. I animated some of your drawings – amazing program Blender is. It's all testing very well.

Rungs said, "Tell him you want to see them. Keep him on line as long as possible. I have a ton of data strings and I have to figure out which one is his."

Picasso2B: Can I see them?

Megaland: Now?

Picasso2B: My stuff has never been animated before. It'd be cool to see.

Megaland: Give me a couple of minutes to load it up.

The sentence lingered on the chat box. The cursor blinked. Rungs was busy reading and capturing the strings of numbers that filled his screen.

"I'm getting somewhere," he said.

Inky looked around his father's study. He stared at the bow and arrow on top of the bookshelf. It was a gift from one of the tribesmen his father had filmed in South America.

He looked away quickly to see that the chat box was filling with text.

Megaland: You there? Let me know when you're ready.

How can I ever be ready for this? Inky thought, looking over at Rungs. But he was anxious to see his drawing come to life.

Picasso2B: Ready.

The screen filled with Inky's drawings. He watched as the basketball dude strutted toward the front of the screen, and the figure he'd dubbed advertising guy pulled out a chair. Then he saw a gift box, which opened itself, leaving wrapping and ribbon on the floor. A strange, silent birthday party. Then the first figure he'd drawn, his Megaland girl based on Amanda, emerged from the box.

Inky was thrilled to see his work on his father's big clear screen. He could see how the computer program had altered and enhanced his originals, and he was thinking what he'd have to do next time to compensate for those effects. The Megaland girl nodded yes and no, leaned forward and back and pointed to what seemed to be the back of a closet filled with shoes. Then the second box appeared, and from it, his Green Goddess.

"Wow," he said, taking in the detail of the dress made of lettuce and spinach leaves.

Rungs got off his chair and stood behind Inky for a closer look. "Way cool," he said.

"Did you get your address?" Inky asked.

"It looks like it's redirecting. Could be something at the provider to manage demand. I'll know when you chat some more."

The Green Goddess stared out at Inky from the screen. He could see Amanda's face in hers. He thought of Amanda that day in the cafeteria when Hawk dragged her away. What had she said to Amanda about him?

Megaland: What do you think?

Picasso2B: I love it. You did a great job, Woody.

Megaland: So did you, Picasso2B. We're a great team.

Inky glanced over at Rungs. He felt a little self-conscious having Rungs see this conversation. But Rungs was more interested in the data than the content, he figured.

Picasso2B: Thanks. Have you shown it to anyone?

Megaland: Your work is having a lot of impact.

Picasso2B: Do you have a lot of testers or is it like one girl somewhere?

Megaland: Interesting question. Why do you ask?

"It's still redirecting," said Rungs. "Slow down between responses. The pauses are good."

Inky typed more slowly, exaggerating his delay between keystrokes.

Picasso2B: Just want to know if I'm any good, I guess.

Megaland: You are very good.

Picasso2B: So like more than one person said so.

Megaland: Marketing research determines user appeal. Your work appeals.

Picasso2B: Cool.

Inky paused before he continued typing, both to appease Rungs and to take in the compliment.

"Bleeping machine." Rungs said. "IP check says he's using a proxy, and the next test I ran should've shown me a header that leads to the original IP. But I'm getting gibberish." Rungs stood up and looked over Inky's shoulder again.

Picasso2B: Any testers work more than the others?

Megaland: It's all statistical, so responses can be weighted, but you don't want to bias your results. I have a lot riding on this data. You don't want the peccadilloes of one user to get in the way.

Picasso2B: The what? Peccadilloes? Sounds like a creature from the stone age.

Megaland: Lol. The *stoned* age is more like it – the Sixties. It was one of my favorite words in high school.

"You can wrap up if you want," Rungs said, looking up from his laptop.

Picasso2B: So do you need more drawings from me?

Megaland: What you've given me is great. You've gotten the gist of the game. I'll be working on the final frames next.

Picasso2B: I'll look over my stuff and see if I can get you something soon.

Megaland: I'd like that Picasso2B. I'd like that.

"SMHID," Rungs said after Inky signed off. "I'm totally scratching my head in disbelief. His IP address is scrambled."

"What does that mean?" Inky asked.

"Could be a couple of things. Some people use a proxy to get around Internet censorship—like people in China do to get on Facebook, or some countries where copyright stuff blocks Netflix. Sometimes NGOs or dissidents use Tor to keep the government out of their pants, but that's crazy slow. Any reason to think he's part of an international company?"

"No. He said he ran a recording studio in the City. I thought he owned it. He said it went broke."

"Could be that someone else is tapping into his communications and they've got it redirected. Could even be that he's being hacked. But most of time, in the stuff my father does, when someone's address is scrambled, they're hiding something or hiding from someone."

"Maybe you're making too much of this. Maybe it's none of that," Inky said. "Maybe he just doesn't want anyone to steal his ideas."

"From what I saw of the game, there's not too much to steal."

Inky thought about defending the game and his work, but Rungs looked too serious.

Rungs closed his laptop and said, "IDK. But I'm gonna go home and see if I can figure it out."

Inky sat in the beanbag chair after Rungs left, feeling drained, like the mushroom beige color of the chair. Rungs seemed to thrive on all the spying and subterfuge. It made Inky profoundly tired. His eyes closed, and soon he was dreaming. In his dream he saw an image of Amanda—not as Amanda, but as an Indian from one of the tribes his father had filmed. She wore the body paint of hunter-gatherers. In her hand she held a pot, no bigger than a coffee mug, but more squat. Her fingers lifted the fitted lid. When she peered inside, there was a small stick glowing orange and red in parts: embers that she took from home to home.

Inky woke up with a start. He knew absolutely what he would do for his core project. He fired up his father's computer again and began to search for copies of his father's emails about the Awa Indians he'd gone to film in Brazil.

Chapter 24
Peccadilloes

RUNGS NODDED TO THE HOUSEKEEPER and went straight to the workroom. The flashing lights of his father's electronics beckoned, more appealing than any toy store.

He loved it when his father would tell him a bit, but never too much, about a case he was working on. He'd always longed for a case of his own, so when Inky presented him with the mystery of Amanda's haircut and the game, he blew it up, stretching the "what ifs" into ominous truths. He'd never admit it, but at first he didn't disagree when Inky said that maybe he was making all this into more than it was.

But then he discovered the rerouted Internet connection. It would be easy to blame it on the general lameness of a service provider, but that wasn't it. So even if nothing nefarious was going on, it presented an intriguing puzzle, more interesting than his homework, and something to occupy him while his father was away. Rungs set to work.

He opened a fresh document. First he copied all the key data, lining up strings of numbers, guessing the IPs surrounding Megaland. Then he wrote down the facts he knew. *Woody. Recording studio. Megaland game.* The page was not full. He must know more.

The guy knew his way around computers. He was good with 3D programs. He'd posted to boards—that was another clue. Then there was the email from his friend at Dalton with the snip of the posting asking for game testers, the post with the information he'd passed on to Inky. That could tell him something, too.

Rungs searched through his messages and found the months-old email. He copied the post to his page. He laid the message next to the IP information he'd pulled at Inky's house. There were four groupings of numbers, just as there should be. He tried some of the jailbreaks known to unlock the dark net. Even the U.S. government could get into Tor with them, but it wasn't working.

He stared at the numbers for awhile. It seemed to him that someone had taken pains, then and now, to scramble the IP, but it didn't look like he was using proxies purchased from a list, and it wasn't one of the known anonymizers his father's programs could detect. There were plenty of reasons not to use them. Some proxies were super slow. Others came from services run for crooks by crooks, which left you open to as much trouble as the anonymity avoided.

Still, he'd taken pains to write a proprietary piece of code to mask his computer. And it was pretty good. Rungs wanted to know what this guy was hiding and why. But first, he knew, he needed to find out how he was doing it. He rubbed his hands together in excitement.

Rungs had a code cracker program he sometimes played with. It used rudimentary scrambling and substitution. He ran the numbers through the program. It returned a long list of possibilities.

He stared at the page-long list. Running each number through a lookup program would be tedious, time-consuming and more trial and error than deductive reasoning. Monkey at the keyboard stuff. He wanted to think this one out. He could picture sitting in the kitchen with a cup of coffee telling his father just how he'd gone about it, their roles reversed this time, with his father in rapt attention, appreciating Rungs's cleverness. Sweet.

But he wasn't there yet. What else did he know?

Recording studio. Music. What else? "Think, Rungs, think," he said to himself. His father would say everything's important. Even the little things. Especially the little things. That's what makes people individual—the unique things they do, their habits, their quirks—their peccadilloes.

OMFG, bam, Rungs thought. Peccadilloes. Woody had used that word in his chat with Inky.

Said it was from the Sixties. Somewhere in that fact was a clue that would help him crack the code. He put his palms together and lowered his head to thank the universe and ask for guidance in finding his solution.

A recording studio guy would be into music, he figured. He put that together with the Sixties, and on a hunch, Rungs Googled "Sixties music," "popular Sixties songs" and, just because he was dealing with code, "songs with numbers in the title." He copied the top results into a master list. He scrolled down the list: "In the Year 2525" by Zager and Evans; "When I'm Sixty-Four" and "Revolution 9" from The Beatles; "Eight Miles High" by The Byrds; "2000 Light Years from Home" by The Rolling Stones; "If 6 Was 9," by Jimi Hendrix.

That last song sounded like a key to crack a simple cipher. Perhaps that was it: if 6 was 9, the key to how Woody distorted his proxy to obfuscate his IP. Rungs went back to the information he pulled at Inky's. What if he transposed the numbers with the base assumption that 6 equals 9?

Rungs wrote the numbers 1 through 9 in one column. Next to the 6 in the next two columns he wrote 9. If he followed the code, 7 would either be 8 or 1; 8 either 7 or 2. He filled in his two columns and came up with options—Woody's IP was either 96.232.14.62 or 93.767.85.37.

It was late. Rungs was hungry and a little jittery from all the sweet Thai coffee he'd been drinking. But he'd only just begun. Now he was sure that this Woody guy was doing something he didn't want detected. Something more than developing an interactive game.

Armed with the two possible IP addresses, Rungs ran a "Whois" on each one, careful to check all five Regional Internet Registries. When one came up as malformed, he knew he had the key to Woody's identity. Now it was easy. Almost too easy. With some clever tracing and tunneling, Rungs found out the IP hooked back to Megaland Studios. Its owner: William "Woody" Turner. Rungs mentally chided himself. He might have saved himself a bit of trouble if he'd guessed that the guy's studio had been called Megaland. It seemed an unlikely choice for someone covering his identity, which suggested that he didn't think he was doing anything so wrong. Intriguing. Was it ambivalence or self-righteousness?

Even if he'd guessed the studio name, Rungs told himself, he'd still have reasonable doubt, and that was the kind of sloppiness that his father warned against. Procedure, facts, method, it was a discipline in itself, like the Muay Thai kickboxing moves they practiced each morning. Guessing and brainstorming had their place when you were stuck. But, Rungs smiled to himself, he was not stuck. He was only beginning. He decided he'd devote the weekend to looking into William "Woody" Turner.

* * *

On Saturday morning, Rungs started with the broadest search, simultaneously running Google and his father's copy of a proprietary search tool. This Woody guy had a lot of Google juice for an old geezer. The studio must have been hot in its day.

The first couple of pages of results were all the same—album credits, links to Amazon and music databases, references to the studio and the musicians who recorded there, many before Rungs was born.

It was tedious to open them and read them all, but that was the disciplined way. He found links to a couple of photographs of the studio, and several to Woody either working at the studio or posing with musicians. He looked like a menswear model compared to the flamboyantly dressed frontmen he posed with. Rungs dated the pictures as best as he could and saved them to files.

The pictures were a nice break from the tedium of the liner note mentions. His tailbone ached from sitting all day and his head hurt from so much screen time. He scrolled through the next page. More liner notes to check, and some announcements for a talent show. Rungs was frustrated. Somewhere in this list was something useful, but where?

He went for a run and heated some dinner. When he set back to work, he pulled up the screens he'd been working on. He clicked a few pages forward. More liner note mentions, blurbs about a talent contest, and then legalese in documents pertaining to creditors. He bookmarked a few. He found stuff related to Woody's divorce. These he'd read first. His father always said, "The people closest to us know us best—and know us least."

Rungs's eyes crossed at the court notices, useful only for their dates, he thought. He went back to the liner notes results. The list didn't look off in any obvious way, but something was driving him to keep looking. He had a hunch—or maybe just a taste for action. Just a few hours, he promised himself. He'd quit by midnight if nothing else turned up. He clicked on to the next page and scanned it. More of the same.

He sent a bunch of the links to Inky, starting with one from the archives of a music fanzine called *Metal Matters*, and asked him to check them out. He continued to research, following the threads from the article, delving into court records and public records where he could, and looked for Woody's other peccadilloes.

Chapter 25
Inky Feels Betrayed

INKY FLIPPED THROUGH THE DRAWINGS in the big sketchpad his father had bought for him years before. Once he'd been so proud of his drawing of the Central Park carousel. Now he could see how the perspective was off; the toothy carriage horse looked like a reflection in a fun house mirror.

He sat down in the beanbag chair and observed how the morning light hit the paper. He'd read an interview with a famous sculptor who said he let his stone suggest what it wanted to be. Inky cleared his mind, or tried to, to see what the paper wanted his drawing to be.

He drew a long arch, then stared at the space around it. It suggested a neckline of a reclining figure. He penciled in the two bones across the neck. It was definitely a girl. What did he know about girls? That was a subject he didn't want to explore. It was the spring semester just after his father's crash that his classmates began dating for real, and making lists of who they liked and wanted to hook up with. But Inky had retreated into his own grief, neither doing the liking nor being liked. He was on no one's list—invisible like a ghost. Until now.

He drew the lines of a torso, thinking how odd it was that Amanda liked someone who she thought was him, but was really nothing like him at all.

He was interrupted by a text from Rungs and reluctantly set aside his drawing.

Rungs: Megaland dude = megabad. Check link I sent and call me.

Inky had ignored the article Rungs had sent, thinking it would be about an all-ages show or something about how famous Woody had been. He remembered their chat when Woody had said he'd had it all. Probably Rungs had stumbled on evidence of his fame, and that's what he'd meant.

K, Inky texted back. He opened the link and saw that Rungs had sent him to a heavy metal publication—not his thing; metal was only big with the Kimchi Clan at school. As he started to read the article from the archives of a music fanzine called *Metal Matters*, "XTreeme Producer Leaves Session in Cuffs," he realized Rungs did not mean bad in a good way. He maximized the type on his phone and kept reading.

"Crash Mackenzie, lead singer of metal gods XTreeme, told Metal Matters *in an exclusive report that legendary producer Woody Turner was led from his studio in hand-*

cuffs, interrupting the production of the long-awaited comeback recording from XTreeme."

"What?" Inky said aloud even though he was alone. He raced through the information about the time between the band's albums, then focused on the part about Woody.

"Mackenzie reports that Turner was charged with sexual abuse in the second degree. The complaint was filed by former model Vanessa Pearl, now separated from Turner, in conjunction with the couple's divorce proceedings. Pearl charged Turner with consorting with a minor. Sources indicate that minor is none other than the winner of Megaland Studios's Rising Stars contest."

"Turner declined to comment, saying his lawyer 'would have a coronary' if he discussed this matter. Crash Mackenzie told Metal Matters that the band will find a way to finish recording, and predicted Turner would not be stopped by 'some washed up model who is now his ex and jealous that Woody Turner is still attractive, even to a young rising star.' Metal Matters has confirmed that charges against Turner have been filed by the 15-year-old contestant. Turner entered a plea of no contest."

What was Rungs trying to do? Whatever had happened between Woody and his ex-wife was no business of his. These were just people who had kicked Woody when he was down; he was trying to make a comeback with this XTreeme band.

Inky felt a wave of nausea come over him. He read the article over again, not skipping over anything this time. How awful. Imagine, the person closest to you turning you in! Didn't the article say his ex-wife was jealous?

Sometimes people were like vultures. He'd have to set Rungs straight. He should know better than to believe everything he read, especially on the Internet.

But when Inky called, Rungs didn't give him a chance. "Meet me at 25th and Lex at ten and we'll talk about it. I can't believe who we're dealing with."

* * *

Inky quickened his pace when he saw Rungs, who was wearing dark sunglasses even though it was a raw and gloomy Sunday. He reminded Inky of a character from a TV movie.

"What's with the shades?" Inky asked.

"Late night. The more I looked, the more I found. This dude . . ."

"You've got it all wrong. Those were just people trying to bring Woody down. It's not like he did any of that stuff."

"DGT, dude. Don't go there."

"What, you can't admit you're wrong?" Inky said.

"Wish I was. He accepted the charges." They had been walking downtown, but Rungs turned east at the corner, in the direction of Amanda's building.

"Well, we don't know the circumstances," Inky said.

"I've seen more than enough. Let me tell you—" Rungs said.

Inky cut him off. "Where are we going?"

"There's a bench with our names on it at the Nth Factor, dude. We have to find out what's really going on with this Woody dude and Amanda."

Inky stopped walking. He hadn't thought about the article in terms of how Woody was acting towards Amanda. He'd been too concerned with the idea that Amanda thought he was Woody to question why Woody wanted to take her picture. How completely lame; here he was all worried about whether she liked him, when he should have connected the dots. But Woody seemed to be such a great guy.

They turned into the courtyard of Amanda's building. Inky sat down reluctantly while Rungs started working with his tricked-out signal finder.

"Let's hope she's like the rest of us and chills on her computer all Sunday," Rungs said.

Inky was not looking forward to spending a gray day on a bench snooping on Amanda's online chat. It made him feel kind of pervy, and he hadn't adopted Rungs's attitude that it was all about the information. He hoped to catch a glimpse of Amanda, maybe have a chance to chat *with* her, although he had no idea what he'd say. And he certainly hoped that the weather would keep the skateboarders away. Running into Hawk would make the day even more completely awful.

"OK," Rungs said, the satisfaction in his voice suggesting some computer success. "Now we wait for her to chat with the creep."

"You don't need to call him a creep. There's more to it than the link you sent," Inky said.

"Oh, is there?" The tone in Rungs's voice sounded sarcastic or pandering.

Inky tried to catch his eye, but he was glancing down at the computer screen. "So he had a thing with a girl who wasn't old enough to do whatever they did. It's not like kids don't sneak into clubs or buy liquor and stuff that the law says they're not old enough to do. Maybe he didn't even know how old she was," Inky said. He couldn't help himself; he had to defend Woody, like he would any friend who was dissed. And the more vigorously he defended him, the more he could stave off the truth.

"An *accidental* creep."

"I read the same article as you. But I know the guy, all right. You don't. He admitted he'd messed up in his life. I even knew about the divorce. Bet you didn't know that, Mr. Detective."

Inky didn't like how Rungs glanced up at him— not with anger at the venom in his words, but with pity. He continued defending Woody.

"He was starting over. This game, it's his second chance. He's trying to make a comeback." There was something about the way Rungs was looking at him that reminded him of how everyone looked at him right after his father's accident. Sympathy like that made him feel like a loser.

"And I was helping. You saw the graphics." As he said that, Inky felt his heart sink. He'd believed in Woody. This all had to be some kind of mistake. He thought the game would be successful. He was counting on it working out.

"Do you think a design-your-dream-date game is really enough to make a comeback?" Rungs asked.

"It's for girls."

Rungs looked down at the computer screen. The silence between them was palpable. Inky had been concerned about his art, but he never really tried the game. He really only knew how Woody thought of it, not what the game was like to play.

"So maybe the game is too lame for us in New York. And we don't really know about girls' games," Inky said. "Besides, people are entitled to try to crawl back out of the hole they dig for themselves."

"The *comeback* creep."

"Stop calling him a creep. He did the crime. He served the time, and now it's over."

Rungs looked up, about to speak, but Inky cut him off and said, "Are you saying you don't believe in second chances? One strike and you're out?"

"Not quite," Rungs said quietly, with that perfect control in his voice. "What you read, that's just what he got busted for."

Rungs pointed at the computer screen. "Here we go." Amanda had signed on to Megaland. Inky was tense, waiting to hear what Rungs had found out.

In a few moments, Amanda was playing a dress-up game. She picked skirts out of an animated closet.

"Check it out. The effects are decent. Good animation, too. " Inky said. "Maybe the game's not that bad."

"Seems your friend Woody has been a busy boy, honing his coding skills and trading pictures on the Internet. Has a particular taste for young girls in pom poms and costumes."

"How can you know that?" Inky asked.

Rungs took off his sunglasses. "I was up all night chasing this stuff down. When you first told me about Amanda getting the haircut you drew, I figured it was Hawk playing a prank on you. Then I liked playing at detective. Unscrambling the IP, that was a nice bit of work. I thought I'd have a good story to tell my dad."

On the screen, the outfits in the closet changed again, and Inky caught a glimpse of his first drawing, now animated. He had to struggle to pay attention to what Rungs was saying.

"But then I probed a little more. I checked out a couple of those pervert sites. My dad has a list of them. Same creeps come to Thailand for sex tourism. Your man was all over the blue sites, plain to see, if you decoded his IP."

They both watched as Amanda selected another outfit and how the model strutted around in it. Despite all that Rungs was saying, Inky liked seeing his drawing come to life, which made him feel incredibly shallow.

"Look. It's serious. I didn't expect it to be. But Woody is a creep. A real creep. You don't have to believe me now. I put together a whole file and emailed a copy to you. Look it over tonight."

On the computer screen, the Megaland chat box appeared. Inky felt his head spin.

Justagirl: I'm going to pick out frames for the photos today.

Megaland: Don't you want to wait for the pictures?

Justagirl: I've seen enough of your work to know you'll do a great job.

As the cursor blinked, Inky slapped the bench. "Just because you draw well doesn't mean you take good pictures," he said to the blinking computer.

Megaland: So we're on for next Saturday then? We can do some pictures for your parents, too.

Justagirl: Great idea.

"He's trying to make her feel safe," Rungs said.

Megaland: Why not surprise them?

Justagirl: I'll just say we're working on a school project.

"Oh man," Rungs said.

Justagirl: They'll be glad that I've made a friend.

Her words stuck through Inky like an arrow. It was like she was flirting through the computer. Flirting with him, even if it was not him. It was all exciting and unfamiliar, and he hated to be robbed of the experience.

But Amanda was agreeing to something that could be very dangerous for her. Just because she felt safe with him.

Chapter 26
Small Places, Large Issues

"I'M GOING NOW," his mother called out. "You gotta get up." Inky slapped at the alarm clock and hit snooze. Monday. "On it," he called. He pulled the blanket over his head and tried to shut out the world.

He woke up again with a start. He was late, but really did have to get to school to tell Rungs he'd read the files he'd sent and Rungs was right. And he really had to talk to Amanda.

He got to school late enough to have to go straight to the principal's office.

Inky sat across from Elsbet Harooni, who asked him the reason for his lateness. Did you ever have a morning when you just didn't want to get up, just couldn't face the day? A day when everything seemed bigger than you, when it is all too much? Inky thought to say. Then he looked at the principal and her perfect hair, and shoes that matched her belt and earrings. He shifted in the uncomfortable little chair. No, she did not have days like that.

"I'm not feeling too well. Headache," Inky told her. It had the benefit of being true.

"This wouldn't have anything to do with your project? I hope you weren't thinking that you could get out of school to put in the work you haven't been doing on your project," the principal said.

Adults were so stupid sometimes. If that's what he'd wanted, he would have just stayed home. Here he actually showed up.

"Nothing like that, Ms. Harooni. It was pretty nasty out Sunday afternoon and I wasn't dressed for it. I think I might have caught something."

"Do you need to see the nurse?"

"No, I just want to get to class," Inky said as the rattan weave poked in his back. He meant it.

"Hurry on then. I'll be attending your project presentation, Michael."

* * *

When Inky slunk into the back of the auditorium, the presentations were already underway. He'd missed Rungs's and felt genuinely bad, although he already knew about the 227 precepts and the custom of becoming a monk before marriage. Now he understood the appeal of being cut off from earthly demands and comforts.

Soon it was Amanda's turn. She was more confident than Inky would have expected as she clicked on her first slide. *Social Structure at the Metropolitan Diplomatic Academy, Upper One*, by Amanda Valdez Bates.

He liked how she'd designed her slides, effective and understated, liked how she tucked her hair behind her ear as she explained in a sweet voice that she was new and was assigned the topic. She'd been to a lot of places, but MDA was much bigger than her other schools and the social dynamic was more complex.

The auditorium was quiet. Inky could feel everyone paying attention—and why not? It was them that Amanda was talking about. He felt a pang of jealousy. Amanda had been the new girl who nobody paid attention to, his and Rungs's little secret. Now she was up there for everyone to see.

"The cafeteria is where it all plays out," Amanda said as she clicked on a diagram of the cafeteria table arrangement. She clicked on the first table on her chart and the name Curry Hill appeared. Everyone giggled.

"Regionalism is set aside for the shared comforts of vegetarian lunches from home generously laced with pungent spices. Don't think this is just the place to find the students who ace their maths. On Curry Hill you'll find the DJ for all the school dances and two thirds of the MDA house band, Fluid Borders. The drummer is part of the Kimchi Clan, known for their infinite variety of heavy metal t-shirts."

One of the boys in the band yelled, "Oh yeah." Amanda smiled. Inky was sorry his seat was so far back.

"There are tables of interest groups," Amanda said, "and several of the tables along the perimeter of the cafeteria were highlighted with their names: the Lab Rats and the Drama Queens." Several students snickered. Everyone used these nicknames about their class, but no one had ever shared them so openly—and in front of teachers.

"The Drama Queens. You would think they'd be part of the Culture Club." When the name appeared, Inky felt himself tense at the mention of his old clique.

"Not anymore. There was a rift in middle school involving the school newspaper," Amanda said.

Inky sucked in his breath. He'd been the cartoonist for years and had his share of run-ins over his columns.

"Seems an article said that this crop of thespians lacked the spark of their predecessors." Inky remembered that, and he could see that Jolene Lee, who'd been the play's lead, did too.

The auditorium grew still. Would Amanda go on about the Culture Club? Would she mention him? There was tension in the air.

"One more thing to know about the Culture Club," Amanda continued. "You'd best stay away from the girls' bathroom around recital time. The prima ballerinas go to great lengths to look their best."

There were a couple of gasps. At least she didn't name names, Inky thought. He saw a bulimic dancer squirm in her seat. "That's not nice," her friend cried out. As everyone turned to look, Inky wondered how Amanda knew all this.

"The Soccer Boys make up the largest group at MDA, and they are a force to be reckoned with." Several of the boys cheered, which broke the tension and caused Mr. Lorenza to tell them to settle down. "They rule by brute force, locker room antics and good looks, if not good grades. MDA is undefeated in soccer again this year."

Inky began to relax. At least she wasn't making trouble for herself. But Inky was secretly disappointed that she passed up a perfectly good opportunity for a dig.

"After the soccer game, they can be found with the girls from the Sacred Circle or the Frenchies. The Sacred Circle girls have the looks, the smarts and the background to reign over the school, and now that they're in Upper School, they finally can. They're in J Brand and Topshop, while the Frenchies emulate their moms in Zara and Chanel. There's movement between the two groups. When one girl ballooned to 150 pounds over the summer, her seat at the Sacred Circle table was no longer available when school resumed. Good thing she was French Canadian."

Amanda looked into the audience in a way that suggested she was expecting a laugh. Instead there was a gasp because everyone knew who she was talking about. Inky could feel the crowd turn. He wondered what had gotten into Amanda. He suspected Hawk.

Amanda seemed less composed as she continued, like one of those actresses at an awards show that rips up her speech to speak from the heart and then bumbles her way into disaster. Her voice dropped and her pace sped up. "But the Sacred Circle can be bribed. After the mom of one of the circle was linked to a certain young and hunky model in the newspaper, it took a walk-on TV role to make it all right in this circle of friends, even though the mom was married and the very young man had been dating—"

From the middle of the auditorium, Priya interrupted. "No. Stop her. She can't talk about that."

"You weren't there. You don't know. You can't talk about my mother like that," Ellen Monahan called out. "You'll get yours, Amanda whatever-your-name-is."

Mr. Lorenza ran up to the podium, while Mrs. Patel escorted Ellen out of the auditorium.

"Thank you, Ms. Valdez Bates. We've heard enough of your report," Mr. Lorenza said as someone turned on the lights.

Inky could see Amanda's face turn bright red. Her face got long, like that Munch painting, *The Scream*. She burst out into tears.

"I'm sorry, I'm sorry," Amanda called out as she raced up the aisle and out of the auditorium.

Chapter 27
Inky Goes to the Glass Tower

INKY LOOKED FOR AMANDA DURING BREAK, but she was nowhere to be found. He tried the roof, the library, the parking lot and the long corridor by the gym. He checked the area around the lower school playground and by the snack machine, stopping to buy some sugar wafers to substitute for lunch. He even went by the guidance counselors' room and peered inside Mr. Lorenza's homeroom. No Amanda.

When the presentations resumed, Inky took a seat in the back and scanned the room. Amanda was still missing. Inky barely listened to the reports. Sven started his presentation by saying "I'm a Soccer Boy, and yes, we're winning again, thank you." Priya and Shiri, who were doing a joint presentation on the meaning of fashion, identified themselves as being part of the Sacred Circle. Poor Amanda. Her report wasn't likely to be forgotten any time soon.

Next, Hawk stepped up to the podium. Inky saw that she was nervous, very out-of-character for Hawk. She pulled at a strand of hair on the side of her neck and wrapped it and unwrapped it around her finger.

Inky wanted to tune out Hawk in support of Amanda. She would never have known any of those stories about their classmates if it weren't for Hawk. Hawk, who was quick to point out others' weaknesses, mishaps and missteps. Hawk, ever strong and unflappable, bright crimson among pastels. Hawk, who made other people miserable because she was unable to cry herself.

Hawk, who reached out to him in need, whose outstretched hand he pushed away.

Her presentation was about social interaction on the cancer ward. The room was quiet, pin-drop quiet. The gladiator shedding her armor.

"Of course, there's not much interaction with the patient. She is pale and gasps for breath. You keep talking, hoping she'll drift into consciousness. You try to imagine her beautiful blond curls. You keep talking, not for her, but for you, because you know that someday soon there'll be no more talking. You keep talking because that's what you're supposed to do, even when you run out of things to say. You keep talking even after the nurse comes in and delivers one of the practiced lies. 'She's a fighter' or 'She's turning a corner now.' That's hospital code for 'She's about to die.'"

The room remained quiet. To Inky, the collective sadness was leaf brown. His head filled with the color of Hawk's loss—and his own.

Hawk described the waiting room at the hospital as "heavy with things unsaid or undone." God, he knew what that felt like.

He resolved that he wasn't going to heap on more regret—he had to talk to Amanda. She needed to know she was in danger, that Woody was trouble and she had bigger things to worry about than a stupid school report.

He raced out of the auditorium as soon as the presentations were over. Principal Harooni caught up with him as he headed towards his locker. "You have a very impressive group of classmates, Michael. I expect that you will rise to the occasion as Helen did."

Ugh, Inky thought. He hated being lumped in with Hawk, a member of the kids-with-dead-parents club. It certainly did not make him want to work on his report.

Seeing the well-wishers begin to gather by Hawk's locker made him feel bad that he was rushing out. He should tell her how brave she was to share as she did, and how much she helped him. But he was focused on Amanda. As he left the building, he dialed the only phone number he had for her—her family's landline. He hung up when her mother's too cheery voice message came on.

He practically raced to Amanda's building, passing by the bench where he and Rungs had discovered Woody's plan to meet her. He hesitated before going inside. The Nth Factor lobby was cold and imposing even to a born New Yorker like Inky. The doorman looked Inky up and down as he approached.

"I'm here to see Amanda Valdez Bates. My name is Michael Kahn."

The doorman scanned a list on his clipboard. "Is she expecting you?"

"No." The doorman's stare made Inky feel like he had to explain himself. "I'm her classmate. She left school early today. I have her homework assignment."

Inky heard only the doorman's end of the conversation. "There's a young man, a Mr. Michaels here to see Miss Amanda."

"Excuse me." Inky felt small. "Not Michaels. Michael Kahn. But she knows me as Inky."

"Mr. Inky," the doorman said into the intercom. There was a pause. "Inky, Inky. Yes, Inky. Has some homework."

The doorman turned to Inky. "They say you can leave the papers with me. They're preparing for guests later."

"It really needs to be explained," Inky said to him, pleading.

The doorman buzzed the intercom again. "He wants to bring it upstairs to explain."

Inky shuffled from foot to foot. The intercom crackled and the doorman picked it up. There was a brief exchange, and the doorman said, "OK, you can go up." Inky felt victorious.

Inky checked himself in the elevator mirror. His reflection did not make him feel more confident. He'd been up most of the night with the files Rungs sent, and it showed on his face. The fuzz over his lip looked like dirt, not like the start of a moustache. His hair was a crazy quilt of lengths.

A housekeeper opened the door. Amanda stood shyly behind. Inky mumbled a greeting and the housekeeper returned to setting the long dining room table, leaving Inky and Amanda in the entranceway.

Everything was new and clean and barely lived in. Inky looked out of the enormous window to the face of a building's clock and the golden dome of an ornate old building. "Cool view," Inky said.

They walked over to the window. Inky's breath fogged the perfectly clean window, and he stepped back. He could see the weave of the fabric in her cocoa colored shirt. Amanda seemed smaller now that he was standing so close to her.

"So what's this homework? Did the teachers assign an essay on screwing up?"

"It's not that bad."

"Why'd you come? I thought you didn't get involved with anyone. Shut yourself down, they say."

"You can't always believe what people say. Or repeat it," Inky said as gently as he could.

"Right," Amanda said and looked down. "All I wanted to do was fit in—all those stories that Hawk told me, she said everyone knew. When everyone started laughing, it was *with* me, and it felt good. It gave me courage to go on, to say more than just what I had written. Then it all slipped out. I never wanted to hurt anyone. Well, maybe Ellen a little. She's always so mean to me."

Inky watched Amanda's face scrunch up as she fought back tears. Inky wanted to hug her to make her feel better, wanted to smooth the lines around her cheeks, wanted to help her stop the sob that was forming in her throat.

He reached out for Amanda's hand. It felt like slow motion as he let his pinky touch her. A tremor of good feeling went through him, yellow and vibrant. A bold color. She did not move her hand away. He placed his fingers over her hand and gently squeezed it.

"I'm sorry," he said. In a moment the sob passed.

"I only wanted to belong. There's no place I fit in. Hawk seemed so sure of herself, I thought . . . I thought she was my friend."

Inky thought about Hawk's presentation, and her description of doing her homework on the cancer ward, and how she waited for her mother to drift into consciousness.

"It's complicated with her. She's been through a lot," he said.

"Funny, she said the same about you. It's awful about your father."

Inky looked down at his feet, then out the window. He knew he was silent for too long. "Can I sit down? Or can we go to your room or something?"

Inky saw Amanda look over to the housekeeper. The flash in her eyes suggested she was asking for permission. Inky wondered if she'd ever had a boy in her room before.

"There wasn't really any homework. I wanted to talk to you."

"My dad's having a dinner party tonight. Fundraising stuff. My mother's out getting her hair done."

"I won't stay long."

Amanda led him down the short hallway. He was expecting her room to be decorated in soft colors and small patterns—calico, and maybe an old quilt, just like you'd see on TV. The bright white walls and furniture and bold geometric print bedspread surprised him, for their design, but also just because he was seeing them. He didn't have much experience in girls' rooms, but he'd guessed the decorating choices were not Amanda's.

He picked up a carved wooden monkey from her dresser. Inky moved its little arms up and down. Amanda bristled.

"Cool," Inky said as he put it down, sensing she was uncomfortable with him touching her things.

"Thanks," she said, softening a bit.

"Listen," Inky said.

"I," Amanda started, speaking at the same time as Inky.

They laughed awkwardly.

Inky noticed that her eyes were red and her face was swollen like she'd been crying for a long time. He wanted to say something to make her feel better. He had so much to say; he felt ready to explode, but he was afraid of saying the wrong thing. He couldn't believe that he was actually alone with Amanda in her room. He forgot the reason he was there for a moment and smiled.

He noticed her hair was no longer parted in the clean lightning bolt pattern of his drawing. The soft part made her hair fall over her face so that he wanted to reach up and brush the hair away.

"I like your new haircut."

"Thanks."

Inky reached for his sketchbook. "Let me show you something."

He sat down on the bed next to her, keeping a polite distance. For him it was close enough to be aware of her body heat. It was thrilling, exquisite, and it made him aware of his own body in a way he never had been before.

He turned to the first drawings he'd done for Megaland and stopped on the page that inspired her haircut. Inky winced as he thought back to the excitement and anticipation he felt when he was drawing it. Innocent and straightforward, he was seizing an opportunity to maybe make something of himself. It was just a couple of weeks or so ago, but now it was all a mess.

He watched Amanda as she looked at the drawing. He compared the curves of her face to the drawing and saw a spot where his lines were off, drawing from memory as he had, and where he had captured her look most accurately.

"I like it better on paper than on the screen," Amanda said.

He could see she was blushing.

"No one's ever drawn me before. It makes me feel special. It's like you really see who I am. I like that the eyes are a little sad."

"That's because we're all a little sad," Inky said softly.

"Well, you should be proud. You're really good. And I'm looking forward to seeing what you do with a camera."

Inky felt himself blush. This was going to be hard. He hadn't really thought out how he'd tell her about Woody and Megaland. About how he knew—and why he cared.

"About that. Yeah. Um, Amanda, it's not what you think. They are my drawings, but it's not me behind the game."

"What?" Amanda draped her arm over her knee and hugged it in and rocked softly.

Inky sat forward. "It's not me you're talking to."

She bit her bottom lip. "I don't know what you're saying."

"How can I explain this?" Inky asked. "Tell me this. How'd you get involved in Megaland?"

"Same way as you."

Inky was not surprised, but he needed the affirmation of his hunch.

"Your friend. My notebook. The first day of school," she said. "When your friend Rungs wrote down the URL for you, the ink leaked through the page, and one night when I was bored, I signed on."

"So you know that I started just the way you did," Inky said.

Amanda looked away. "I, er, I didn't think of that . . ." She looked down at the floor, then the wall. She looked upset, then brightened. "But your drawings?"

"Those are my drawings, but it's not me you're chatting with." Inky saw another flash of concern on her face. "I'm not so into games, that's Rungs's thing. But I wanted to show my work, make up for not going to Art & Design. Do something big."

"And?"

"And instead of testing the game, I asked to draw stuff for it. He liked my work. It was cool to feel like I was part of something—and he was good to chat with. He understood."

"Yeah, I know what you mean," Amanda said.

"It was nice to hear good things about my art, especially with all the crap at school." He paused. "It was like the game let me be another person."

"I totally understand."

There was something in her tone of voice and her exaggerated nod that made Inky think she heard something he wasn't saying. "Not really that, exactly," he said.

"I used to hate this school. I thought everyone was stuck up and mean. And all the groups. I thought no one would be nice to me," Amanda said, moving closer to him. "Now I don't hate it so much."

Inky wanted to stay in that moment. He wanted to hug her for real. Maybe he could tell her the rest about Woody and Megaland another time.

"Chatting with you made it easier," Amanda said softly. Inky realized that she still didn't accept that he wasn't Woody. Inky shuddered. He had to get her to believe the truth.

"It's not me. You're chatting with a guy named Woody Turner. I know he's gonna take your picture. But you have the wrong idea about him. He's not a nice guy."

Amanda got up and walked over to her dresser. She wound up the little mouse and let it dance across the surface.

"I think he's very nice," Amanda said with a laugh. "It'll be the perfect present. Especially with my new haircut—thanks to what you saw in me."

Inky was so flustered he sputtered his words. "It was you that I based my drawings on, the drawings you saw on Megaland. But I'm not Woody," Inky said.

"Woody is an older guy and he likes young girls. Likes them to dress up—cheerleaders' outfits and stuff—and do pervy things. He's been arrested because of it, and he's using this game to get to you."

Amanda turned towards him sharply. As she braced herself on the dresser, she knocked the little mouse to the floor. "Why are you saying this? Why won't you admit you liked chatting with me, too?"

Inky got up and walked towards her. She crossed over to the other side of the room. "I get it. It's because of my presentation. I crossed Ellen Monahan and now no one wants to have anything to do with me. This is just your way of getting out of it."

"Amanda, that's not it at all. I don't care about Ellen frickin' Monahan. She had it coming anyway. I care about . . ." Inky realized he was shouting and lowered his voice. "I care about you knowing the truth about Megaland. What I'm telling you is true."

He was acutely aware that he'd almost told her that he liked her, which made little sweat beads form around his forehead and over his lip. He wiped his finger across his lip and hoped she didn't notice.

"You're lying." She glared at him and sat down at her desk. "It has to be you I'm chatting with. How else would you know about the photo session?"

Inky wished the floor would swallow him up. His emotions were sharp-edged rays of molten orange slicing through him. The room spun. He had to tell her the truth.

"Rungs and I saw you. He hacked your computer and saw your chat with Woody."

"What?" Amanda bolted out of the chair. "How?"

"Rungs is kind of a genius at that stuff. That revised rubric document he sent you—that was a key to get into your computer."

"I don't believe it. This can't be true. Are you telling me that he spied on me? That you spied on me?"

Inky nodded and opened his mouth to explain.

"That's illegal and creepy. It's none of your business who I meet or what I do on my computer." Amanda jumped up. "What's it to you?"

"Look, the guy suggested you come to his studio so he could take pictures of you," Inky said. "Does that sound like a part of beta testing a computer game or more like you're part of his game?"

"That's disgusting. You're just jealous that it's not you. I don't want to have anything to do with you or your Thai spy friend."

"Amanda . . ." Inky stood up and walked over to her.

"This whole school is messed up, and the two of you most of all."

"But Amanda . . ."

She cut him off. "You should go now." She pushed him out of her room and walked him to the door. "You should go and never talk to me again. Goodbye."

Chapter 28
Keep the Home Fires Burning

EVERYTHING WAS WRONG, INKY THOUGHT, as he sank into the beanbag chair in his father's study. He'd blown it with Amanda. He had done nothing to keep her out of danger, and now she hated him on top of it. How creepy was it that Woody was using his drawings to lure her in? Who knew, maybe he was using them on other girls, too? Rungs would probably be pissed that Inky went to Amanda's without him. And then there was his school project, which was due in just a couple of days. Even Amanda's failure had been well prepared and well rehearsed.

If he flunked this project, he felt like he'd be disappointing his father. Ever since Rungs talked about the *pii*, the spirits, whatever it was, Inky thought he felt his father watching him. And without a good grade on this project, he'd likely be tossed out of school and could kiss any thoughts of a decent college goodbye. Ms. Harooni's voice echoed in his head. He was expected to do something impressive.

The pressure literally made his right hand lock up. Art had always come to him easily, naturally. Why, with everything else in his life so hard, did he have to be stuck now?

Inky pulled out his oversized sketchpad. The white paper seemed to stare at him, accusatory in its blankness. He made a quick angry line across the top third of the page. "Be something, anything," he said to the page.

His shoulders rolled back as he thought of the view from Amanda's window, his sharp line the horizon at dusk. He thought of the ornate clock they'd seen from her window, and penciled in a line. Probably she'd be in her room now, shunted aside while her parents had their dinner party. He wished he'd asked her for her IM. But she wouldn't have chatted with him anyway.

He stepped back from his page. The line was all wrong, soft where it should be bold. Rather than a cityscape, it suggested a shoulder. He drew in a torso, working swiftly and confidently, his lines ripe as fruit. He continued to work, breathing life into the page. He narrowed the line by the hipbone, and thought of Amanda's long legs.

Inky wondered if she'd sign on to Megaland. For a second, he thought to ask Rungs to spy on her. Ugh. This had all gone too far.

He set aside his sketchpad and looked around the study. The wooden mask on the shelf looked down at him, swirls of orange paint accentuating the eyeholes. A witness to his uncertainty. He remembered how excited his father had been before that last trip. He said it was the chance of a lifetime to film a previously unknown tribe, his duty to bear witness.

When Inky was little, his father often took him to the lower level of Grand Central Station. They'd sit in the oversized maroon and green chairs and look at the intricate designs on the wall. Sometimes they'd grab a snack and sit at the wondrous tables with tops made of laminated tickets and mementos from train trips past. They'd make up stories about the people who passed by, then his dad would cover the tables with blank paper and say, "Draw what you see." Or "What color does it feel like today?"

Behind the tables were enormous lightboxes of photographs. "There's nothing better than a public display to get your message out. Someday, it could be your work up here for everyone to see."

It might not be in lightboxes, but he could make a public display.

Inky lined up some bottles of drawing ink, lush green and woody brown—the colors of the jungle. He began to imagine the scenes his father must have seen. He thought of feathers, peacock blue and scarlet red, maybe a bright yellow. He filled his little tub with water; to get the tone of Indian skin right, he'd have to mix the color himself.

He took out the block of Arches paper his father had bought him a couple of years ago. He ran his finger over the calligraphic script on the cover, which said the paper was milled in France since 1492. The paper of serious artists. Suitable for framing. Inky switched on the radio and started to hum.

He rubbed his finger on the embossed corner, set down a sheet of paper, felt its thickness, its tooth, and let the soft white speak to him.

Chapter 29
The Fog Rolls In

AMANDA STARED OUT THE WINDOW, too overwhelmed to do anything else. Too much had happened that day. The weather was turning; a gray mist swallowed the building spires. Her report had started out fine. Why hadn't she just basked in that feeling, like a lizard in the sun? Why didn't she just go on with her report as she'd prepared it? If she'd just stuck to the script, maybe she wouldn't be the hated mean girl; maybe Inky would still be her friend, or almost friend, or whatever he'd been. But then she wouldn't have found out how sneaky he was—snooping on her with his spyboy friend.

Could it be true? Was there really a creepy guy behind Megaland, or was Inky just making that up? Hawk said he was a strange one. Maybe he had a fight with someone at the game about his artwork or something, and this was just revenge.

But what if Inky was right and she'd been chatting with some dangerous guy? Who was this

Woody, anyway? She couldn't exactly ask Woody if he was a creep, but maybe there were other things she could find out.

Amanda signed on to Megaland. The home page appeared, and she immediately felt the storm within her subside. She liked having this special place, a little mindless amusement and the chance to chat with someone she found easy to talk to. It made her sad that it would never be the same. The chat box opened.

Megaland: Welcome back Justagirl. Do you want to see the new scenarios for the game?

Amanda wondered how he knew to sign on when she did. Did his computer make a sound, like when you get a new email, to let him know that someone signed on to the game? How did he know it was her? Were there other girls? Did they have each have their own special sound? All of a sudden Amanda was nervous. She hadn't planned what she was going to say. When in doubt, try the truth, her father often said.

Justagirl: I don't feel much like playing. I bombed my report today.

Megaland: Maybe playing will take your mind off of it.

Justagirl: I just feel like chatting.

Megaland: OK. So tell me, did you totally bomb or were there good parts?

Justagirl: There was good stuff. Usually I'm scared to talk in front of a group, but I practiced and it felt OK. Then I got into it and started talking. I said some things I shouldn't have. I hurt someone.

Megaland: That must hurt you, too. I know it can be very hard to pick up after you've made a mistake.

Zut, Amanda thought. This wasn't how it was supposed to go. Still, chatting with him was making her feel better.

Justagirl: At least I know I won't make the same mistake again. I'll just stick to what I planned.

Megaland: Don't be too hard on yourself. It's tough not to repeat mistakes.

Amanda thought about that for a moment. It was one of those wisdom things adults say, but she thought he might be talking about himself, too.

Justagirl: Does that happen to u? Do u make the same mistakes?

The cursor blinked. It seemed to take him longer than usual to reply. Was she on to something?

Megaland: Change is very hard.

Amanda didn't reply right away. She was curious what else he might say.

Megaland: But don't you worry, maybe your teacher saw all the good things in your report.

It felt like he closed down. Was this all she'd get to work with to figure out who he was?

Justagirl: Not. He didn't even let me finish.

Megaland: Life is filled with surprises - like the pictures you have in store for your family. Think about that.

Amanda couldn't help but notice how he'd changed the topic. Now maybe she could get him to say something that would show his true intentions. But what?

Justagirl: I'm looking forward to that. What will it be like?

Megaland: What do you want to know?

Justagirl: Oh, everything. What I should wear, what I should do.

Again, there was a hesitation. She bit her lip until it hurt.

Megaland: Oh dear, that's a lot of questions. Don't worry about what you're going to wear; there will be lots of costumes to choose from. The pictures will be beautiful, because you are.

Justagirl: Why do you say that? You don't know what I look like.

Megaland: I know this much, you're a beautiful person. That will show through in the pictures.

Justagirl: IDK, but tnx.

Amanda smiled at using one of the abbreviations Hawk had taught her.

Megaland: Well, I do know. I think I know you rather well, Justagirl. But I don't know which costume you would pick. Perhaps you'd like to be a cheerleader? Pride in your new school and all. Would you like that?

Merde. Sacrebleu. He was talking about a cheerleader costume. Hadn't Inky told her he liked girls to dress up like cheerleaders? Her hand started shaking as she started to type a response. The guy behind Megaland really was a creep. Inky was right. But how could it be? She was too smart to have this happen to her.

Justagirl: A cheerleader? I'll have to think about that.

Justagirl: I guess I have all week to think about who I want to become.

Chapter 30
Making Contact

"**M**ICHAEL KAHN WILL TELL US ABOUT 'Caste, Costume and Custom,'" Mrs. Patel announced from the podium.

Dang, Inky thought as he approached the microphone. He'd forgotten to tell his teacher that he changed his topic. Mrs. Patel hated surprises.

"I, er, hello, everybody. I am Michael Kahn, but I'm not going to talk about costume or custom. What I'm going to present to you today is called 'Making Contact.'"

Inky saw Principal Harooni pucker her lips like she'd bit into a lemon. She glowered at him. Inky took a deep breath. He clicked on his first slide. It was the long text of an email. He magnified the first paragraph and read the words as they appeared on screen.

"'Ted, I have the most extraordinary news. I've found a previously uncontacted tribe of Indians.'"

Inky could see Rungs in the middle of the auditorium. He gave Inky a thumbs up.

"And so it began," Inky said. "That email was from Raoul Costa to his college roommate, a documentary filmmaker. Costa is an officer in FUNAI, the Indian land rights organization in Brazil."

Inky clicked to the next slide. He lowered his voice and moved closer to the microphone so it sounded like the pleading whisper he imagined would be Raoul's tone if he was reading the words.

"'There are very few of them, you must come and document how they live. I can offer you harsh conditions, bad food, excellent company, only minimal upfront funding, and a chance to make history. Old friend, I need you. The loggers are encroaching on the Indian's hunting land. Come soon. You must prove they exist so we can protect them. You must bear witness.'"

Principal Harooni still had her lemon face, but at least she was paying attention. Inky continued. "It promised to be a new and exciting chapter in the career of the filmmaker," Inky said, with one hand tightly gripping the podium. "It turned out to be the final chapter in his life."

Inky's voice cracked, but he continued. "That documentary filmmaker was my father, Ted Kahn, who died in a plane crash returning from filming a newly discovered branch of the Awa Indians in the Brazilian Amazon. His film perished along with him. Today I'm telling the story he never got to tell."

Inky looked out into the auditorium. He scanned the audience for Amanda. The dim lights made it hard to see faces. Hawk caught his eye and nodded from her seat near the front. Inky found that oddly comforting.

He switched to a slide of one of the images he had drawn. It was of a headband hanging from a branch, its bright feathers a contrast to the greens and browns of the jungle background. He liked how the brightly-colored drawing inks held their saturation on the enlarged slide.

"Raoul's job is to survey the Indian population. He looks for signs of their campsites and marks off their land to keep out gold diggers and loggers and exposure to disease. The Indians in that region are hunter-gatherers; they move to their food source, some seasonally, some more frequently. He's familiar with the language and symbols of most of the tribes.

"One day he found a headband, like this one, caught in the branches of a low jungle bush. It was a patterned headband with bright orange toucan plumage and yellow and red macaw feathers. He did not recognize the pattern as the work of any of the Indian tribes he was familiar with in the area. Raoul kept the headband attached to his canteen strap as he continued to traipse through the jungle looking for signs of Indian activity, his loose kind of census."

Inky switched the slide. The image on the screen was a forest scene, seen from the perspective of someone on the ground looking up. In the treetops two pairs of eyes and two mouths were visible. The lines of the bodies were woven into the pattern of the foliage. It was an artfully done image, Inky thought with some satisfaction. The medium-nibbed pen had been the right choice. He continued to tell the story.

"One day, Raoul heard whispering coming from a tree above him. He knew he was being watched as he set up his camp for the evening. He made his food and pitched his tent. He let the Indians watch him. He was not afraid.

"In the morning, they were still there, or there again. Raoul packed up his things, then looked up in their direction. He knew they saw him, and felt that he'd caught their eyes."

Inky changed the slide to one that was meant to be Raoul, as if viewed from the trees above. It showed him placing the headband on the ground.

"Raoul kept eye contact with the Indians as he placed the headband down by where his tent had been, and walked away towards a clearing. He did not turn around to see if they retrieved it."

The next slide was his rendering of a giant tortoise that filled the screen. He looked out into the audience, this time seeing that Mrs. Patel and Mr. Lorenza both appeared to be interested. He quickly scanned the right side of the room. No Amanda.

"The Indians tracked down Raoul several days later. They brought a gift to his campsite. A giant tortoise. It was a valuable gift. Tortoise is an important food to a nomadic tribe; it could be stored live on a giant rack. The headband Raoul had found belonged to one of the tribe's elders, and the gift honored him for its return."

Inky switched the slide to a drawing of a tribal ceremony. The Indian men wore their lip plugs and body paint; the women were by the fire, tending to packets of food wrapped in giant green leaves. Inky explained the slide.

"Raoul was eventually invited to a ceremony. He called it a 'moving on' ceremony, as it coincided with the tribe breaking down camp and moving to another hunting location. I imagine a ceremony like that is the last thing that my father filmed."

Inky paused for a second. His throat tightened. He fought back tears. He switched to the next slide. It reminded him a little of a Chagall print his father had taken him to see. It was his favorite drawing in the series. The image was of the Indians dancing around the fire, a swirl of bodies, their boundaries merging in a ghostly blur. To the side, where his father might have been seated, was the camera, and instead of his father's face behind it, Inky had drawn his own.

"The ceremony was a way to offer thanks to the site for giving them the food that would get them through the season."

Inky switched to a slide that showed a rack of tortoises and stacked packets of food for the tribe. Principal Harooni had dropped her pucker face, and she was leaning forward in her seat. Inky was coming to the end of his presentation. He scanned the lower left side of the auditorium. No Amanda.

"When the feasting and dancing was done, the campsite was broken down."

Inky clicked on to his last slide. It showed a small vase-like vessel encased in a holster of animal skin and rope. It was decorated with the same pattern and bright colors as the headband. Inky looked up towards the middle of the left side of the auditorium. There was a cluster of Soccer Boys.

He wanted Amanda to see this slide. He knew she'd understand it. Where was she?

"Before the tribe puts out the fire, one of the women scoops up a cupful of embers from the fire and places them in a special pot."

He let his eyes scan the back left of the auditorium, making it seem like he'd paused for effect. He found her all the way in the back and caught her eye. She looked down.

"This ember pot would be brought with them to their next campsite. The embers from the fire in their last home would be used to start the fire in the next."

Inky saw that Amanda was looking up at him. He struggled to read her expression. It was hard to see with the lights dimmed. Someone coughed. He knew he was pausing too long.

"Time is running out for the Indians in the Amazon. Gold has been discovered on some of the tribal lands. Mining will certainly ruin the habitat of the animals they hunt. Each year more and more acres are lost to illegal logging."

"So we see the Awa Indians of the Amazon carrying their fire from spot to dwindling spot, giving thanks for what they have, rather than mourning what they've lost."

Inky closed his eyes for a split second, hearing his own words. How proud he was of his father's journey.

When he started to speak again, his voice cracked. "The ember pot may look like a trinket you'd put on a dresser," Inky said, thinking of being in Amanda's room, "a reminder of a faraway place."

He paused once more for effect and tried to hold Amanda's gaze. "For the Awa, and maybe for all of us, it is a reminder that home is made from the sparks you carry."

Chapter 31
What You Don't See

IT SEEMED LIKE FOREVER UNTIL MR. LORENZA and Mrs. Patel thanked the students in the core program for their presentations. Principal Harooni got up and told them what fine examples of the Metropolitan Diplomatic Academy tradition they were. "You came through for me, even the students who got off to a rocky start." Inky's cheeks burned.

He was glad it was over. All the intense drawing he'd done over the past few days left his shoulders aching from hunching over the paper. His fingers were tight and crampy. It felt like it should be the end of the year, not just the first trimester. All he could think about was taking a nap as soon as he got home.

"Nice job, Artboy," Hawk called out across the hallway. Inky was too wrung out to do anything more than smile.

"Ditto," Rungs said. Then quietly he added, "He would have been proud."

Inky felt the twinge of tears forming. Even though Rungs had come to MDA last year and never knew his father, he was right. How he wished his father was there to tell him so. He peered into his locker, not so much to find anything, but to compose himself.

"XME for changing the subject, dude, excuse me. But we have to get on the case with Megaland, ASAP," Rungs said.

"Now? Not now," Inky said, taking his jacket out of his locker and raising his head up to look at Rungs, who was grinning.

"Well, maybe not right now," Rungs said, gesturing with his chin to Amanda approaching them from the far hallway.

Inky put his jacket back in the locker; he felt clammy. She had a right to be mad at him for spying on her—even if it was for a good reason.

"Listen, I . . ." Amanda said.

"No, I . . ." Inky said at the same time. He noticed the part in her hair was back to its lightning-bolt pattern.

They laughed, and Inky thought back to his visit to Amanda's apartment when the same thing happened.

"Your report. It was really good. I loved what you said about carrying home from place to place. So poetic."

Inky was only conscious of Amanda. He no longer felt like he was in the MDA hallway, was no longer aware of the row of lockers and his classmates gathering their jackets and books, barely conscious that Rungs had stepped away. It was just Amanda.

That was a new sensation for him. He'd never been able to turn off the visuals around him before. What he saw had always influenced what he thought. Now, what mattered was what was in his heart. Inky pushed his shoulders back and raised his head.

"I was thinking of you when I wrote that," Inky said.

Amanda blushed, and Inky loved the color of it—a soft pink of early dusk washed over her cheeks.

"I'm sorry about the other day," she said. "First, I thought you were playing a trick on me, and I was already messed up from my report. Then, I guess I just couldn't believe that someone who'd been so nice was a pervert."

"What made you change your mind?" Inky asked.

"When I read through all the links and saw what he'd done."

"Links?" Inky hadn't sent her any links. He didn't even have her email address.

"Rungs sent them to me. Said I needed to see for myself."

Inky felt a pang of jealousy that Rungs sent something to Amanda without telling him. Then he remembered he'd ignored Rungs's calls for days while he'd immersed himself in his project.

"I can't believe what he did to that girl," Amanda said. "She entered a contest. She trusted him to help her with her singing career."

"Like we trusted him," Inky said, no longer inclined to defend Woody.

Rungs returned to where Inky and Amanda were standing.

"We gotta talk about what we're going to do. Let's go to your place," Rungs said to Inky. Then he turned to Amanda. "Together we should be able to figure something out."

Amanda nodded, not saying yes, but walking with Inky and Rungs out of school.

"All right," Rungs said. "We're gonna bring your guy Woody down."

Chapter 32
Size Matters

INKY WAS NERVOUS ABOUT WHAT AMANDA would think of his apartment. The old four-story brick building was such a contrast to the ritzy, glass monolith she lived in. As they turned the corner to his block, Inky stumbled on the sidewalk where an old tree root lifted the pavement.

"We are so gonna get him. We're ITC here. In total control," Rungs said, grabbing them both. Inky smiled and watched Rungs shift into his alpha personality. Then he stole a glance at Amanda and smiled some more.

When they entered his father's study, Inky saw Amanda look first at the drawings scattered on the floor. Inky had finished the final scans for his school project that morning. He hadn't expected company.

"Cool," Amanda said going over to the pile of drawings. "May I?"

Inky could almost feel the touch of her slender fingers as she carefully considered each image, and then turned them face down in an orderly pile. When she came to the drawing on the bottom, Inky turned as red as the lips on his sketches. It was the piece he'd started working on when they'd first discovered something was not right with Megaland— nothing more than the outlines of a young woman's body.

"I, er, didn't get very far," Inky said.

"You chat with Woody again? Did he say anything more about meeting you?" Rungs asked.

Amanda seemed flustered. "Yes. I mean, I had to know for myself. Before you sent me the links."

"And," Rungs said.

Inky was bothered by Rungs's question. He saw the light pink flush of Amanda's cheeks intensify.

"And she's here," Inky said.

Amanda looked up from the drawings and smiled. "These are really good."

"Did he ask you anything, um, inappropriate?" Rungs said.

Amanda got up and walked to the window. She looked out at the tree. Inky wondered what it was that she was considering.

Softly and without turning to face Inky or Rungs, Amanda said, "Yeah. He asked me if I'd put on a cheerleader's outfit for the pictures."

Inky's stomach did a flip and his head filled with the ruby-hot color of danger.

"That's awful," Inky said. He expected Rungs to also be outraged and shocked, but his expression didn't change. Amanda noticed, too.

"Did you know that?" Amanda asked Rungs. Inky was surprised at how direct she was.

"Not very imaginative, this Woody," Rungs said.

Amanda stared at Rungs for a moment. "No answer?" His face didn't change.

"I should call you Spyboy," she said. "It'll be Spyboy and Artboy."

"Are you mad?" Rungs asked earnestly.

"I was."

"But you're not still?" Inky piped in.

Amanda looked at him and Inky felt like jelly inside. "You know, no one ever cared enough about me to spy on me," she said. "In Nairobi, my brother Derek had a girlfriend. I used to listen in on their conversations. I guess I was worried that she'd take him away from me. She was from town, not our school, and with all the political trouble, I guess I was scared for him, too."

"What happened?" Inky asked.

"Same thing as always. We moved."

Inky laughed. "So you're not mad, or do we have to move away?"

"Oh, don't move," Amanda said. "I'm just getting to know you."

Inky felt like the azure blue of a perfect fall morning. The fatigue from working on his project faded.

"CFD, it's time to call for discussion—since we're all staying," Rungs said. "If we want to get Woody, we have to have something concrete on him."

Inky didn't want to hear it. He wanted to show his drawings to Amanda, not think about Megaland and how Woody wanted to dress Amanda as a cheerleader. "Can't we let the police figure that out?"

Rungs shot him a withering look. "They're not gonna do anything if we don't have evidence. But we totally can—assuming Amanda helps us."

They both looked over to Amanda. "If I can, I guess. OK," she said.

Rungs caught her eye and held her gaze, like he was sizing her up. "OK. What we have to do is get Woody away from his computer and camera, after he's taken pictures of Amanda."

Whoa. Inky felt like he'd been slapped in the face by a winter wind. He wasn't so sure about Rungs's idea. Maybe Amanda could just not show up and someone else could bust the guy. He would gladly draw her picture for her Christmas present for her brothers.

That was it. When did Rungs get a superhero cape? He wasn't the only one who could hatch a plan. He picked up the big unfinished drawing and looked at it as if he saw more than the lines on the page. Inky's fingers smarted from the past few days of non-stop effort. He laid the drawing out on his father's desk, reached for his pencils and willed his aching fingers into action.

"Now? You're drawing now?" Rungs asked.

"I have an idea," Inky said.

Rungs stuck out a cupped hand and pretended it was a microphone. "Tell us your idea, Mr. Artboy."

Amanda clapped her hands appreciatively, which made Inky less annoyed. When she clapped, her breastbone curved in a way that emphasized the strong definition of her neck. She was more than zebra pretty. She was beautiful.

"Woody tried to lure Amanda using my art right?"

Amanda and Rungs both nodded.

"I'll lure him away from his computer with a drawing just for him."

Inky could almost hear Rungs trying to figure out his plan. Amanda looked at him expectantly.

"He likes young girls, right? I'll draw him a girl he'll really want. Then I'll upload just a piece of it and get him all interested."

Inky stood up and pointed to the poster-sized paper on the big desk. "But it'll be too big to scan, so I'll bring it to him. And when will I drop it off? When Amanda is there, of course."

Rungs bowed a half-bow in honor of Inky's plan. "WOA. It's a work of art."

Inky looked over at Amanda and saw she was nodding her approval. He had to admit, it was clever.

He picked up the drawing from the floor, set it on the desk and took out his box of colored pencils and pastels. Amanda settled into the beanbag chair under the window. Inky was not used to working in front of other people. Even in art class Inky would go off to a corner of the room.

But there was no time for that now. Inky thought of the caricaturists hawking their sketches to tourists at the Central Park entrance by the Plaza, capturing images in a few sure lines. His favorite birthday party was when his father brought Inky and his friends there for portraits and a picnic. His father had always made a big thing about his birthday, but he understood now it was his choice; he enjoyed it, too. It was Woody who helped him realize that. This was some way to thank him.

Amanda thumbed through a book and Rungs seemed lost in thought. Inky refocused on his drawing and still felt self-conscious that he was working on a nude—and with Amanda in the room. He wondered if she thought the body resembled hers. He pushed the thought out of his head. He just had to keep working.

"Can I have your barrette?" Rungs asked Amanda.

"This?" she said as her hand touched her butterfly hairclip. Rungs nodded and Amanda removed the hairclip and handed it to him. "Why?"

"All the better to hear you with, my dear," Rungs said. "I want to see if we can fit a microphone in there." He examined the butterfly.

"Microphone?" Amanda asked.

"Yeah. An omni-directional mic. We want to be able to hear your conversation, and an omni'll pick up sounds from any direction. You've seen those mics the TV guys clip on their jackets? Like that."

Inky looked up from his work to Amanda seated under the window. He reached for light, bright colors.

But the lightness faded quickly. "And where are we going to be?" he asked Rungs.

"Working on it," Rungs said.

"It's too dangerous for her to be there alone," Inky said.

"We can do this. Together we can do this. Just hear me out," Rungs said.

Inky was still concerned, but he figured he owed it to his friend to at least listen. Plus, he was swept up by Rungs's enthusiasm. It felt good to belong to something, strange as this all was, and he didn't entirely mind the fatherly way Rungs was speaking.

"So, yeah. You have to wear a mic," Rungs said to Amanda. "One thing for sure, you don't want to wear silk or polyester. Too much rustle. We won't be able to hear a thing."

That gave Inky an idea. He sketched an outline of a silk scarf in turquoise pastels and draped the line provocatively across his drawing's shoulder. Amanda got up and looked at his work.

"You'll need to wear cotton or wool, and you don't want the mic next to your skin. Sweat and body oil are the enemies of wireless transmission," Rungs said.

Inky laughed, mostly because the mention of body oil and sweat made him self-conscious with Amanda so close by. "Is that so, Spyboy?"

Amanda giggled. Her laugh was the color of violets. But Inky's mind was still filled with a murky gray. "I'm not getting how we listen to whatever the ominous microphone picks up," he said, trying to keep his voice even, but feeling concern for Amanda's safety.

"That's omni-directional—not ominous—and I'm working on it. I'll see what my dad has. We need something with some range. Then we'll see how far away we can be."

Inky scanned Amanda's face for any signs of concern or fear. She was concentrating, like she was studying for a test. She looked serious, but not outwardly afraid—less nervous-looking than when she first sat down with them in the cafeteria. That actually made him more nervous.

"Maybe this isn't such a good idea. Maybe we should call the police," he said.

"And say what?" Rungs said sharply. "That we know this guy who violated his parole by chatting with an underage girl about a game he's designing. And how do we know this? We hacked into his computer. With a good lawyer, he'd beat the charge, no problem."

"Maybe there's nothing to this, then. If Amanda doesn't go, then there's no real problem. Leave him to his lame game. It's not like he's a robber or psycho-killer or something," Inky said.

"No real problem? Don't you get it? When my father busted the Thai sex tourist ring, all those guys were like captains of industry. They don't really think they're doing anything wrong, so they do it over and over again."

"That's messed up," Inky said, looking over at Amanda.

"How is Woody any different? He used your art to get close to Amanda."

Amanda's lips were scrunched in anger. "He's a phony and a fake and a bad man. I really thought he was OK—a friend. You know . . ." Amanda pointed her chin towards Inky, "like you. But all he wants is to see me in some little outfit. It's sick and I hate him and I want us to stop him."

She was right. Woody was heinous, and Inky was embarrassed for his concern over getting credit for having his drawings in Woody's game. Now he was drawing something that mattered. "We're in the perfect position because he has no idea that we know each other," he said.

"Amen," Rungs said. "We just have to get enough on him so when we do call the police to bust him, it's gonna stick."

The calling the police part made Inky feel a little better, but he was still shaky inside. He didn't want to seem like a coward, so he just kept drawing. He waited for Amanda to say something.

"I want to do this. I really think we can," she said.

There was nothing else for him to say. He wondered, was she that brave? Or didn't she see the risk? And then his thoughts shifted. Was he brave enough?

A year ago he wouldn't have cared about doing anything dangerous—what had there been to look forward to? To live for? He'd been caught up in feeling that all was lost. But now, now, he looked over at Amanda, then over to Rungs. He thought about his mother. There was so much at stake. Inky tried to picture exactly how it would play out, but he couldn't.

"There's still something I don't get. Where are we going to be when Amanda first goes in? How do I know when to deliver the picture? Are we just going to stand on the street? What if there's traffic? Or construction? How will we hear over that?" he asked.

"I'm gonna check it out tomorrow to see if there's a spot within range where we can hang out," Rungs said.

"If it rains or something, we're screwed. Too bad we don't have a car," Inky said.

"Bingo," Rungs said. "A cab. We can pay the driver to not go anywhere."

"That's hardly clandestine," Inky said.

Amanda chimed in. "I have an idea."

"And it could be expensive," Inky continued. "The meter would be running the whole time."

"I really do have an idea," Amanda repeated, sounding annoyed. "Hawk's driver."

Inky and Rungs exchanged looks.

"Wait, wait, don't say anything," Amanda said, holding a hand up toward them. "Just listen. The way I see it, she owes me. If it wasn't for all her stories, I wouldn't have messed up my report. She said it was all stuff that everyone knew. Old news. She forgot to say how much everyone still cared." Amanda's voice broke up.

"Her father lets her use the driver to go anywhere she wants. We went to Jackson Heights one night because she wanted me to try some special curry puffs. And the driver doubles as her father's bodyguard."

"No way Hawk's involved," Inky said.

"IMO, we need that car," Rungs said, "but that's just my opinion. We should all agree."

"It'd make me feel a lot safer. I'm the one going in first," Amanda said.

They looked at Inky. He concentrated on his drawing and said nothing.

"Someone else should know about this in case something goes wrong," Amanda said.

"We need that car. And there's more to her than mean girl—her report and all," Rungs said.

"OK," Inky said to Amanda. "Ask her." He hoped Hawk would come through for them, even though he hadn't been there for her.

Chapter 33
Can't Say No

INKY COULD STILL FEEL THE PRESENCE of Amanda and Rungs in his father's study long after they'd gone. His drawing was complete enough to set their plan in motion.

He scanned the corner section that showed the top curve of a breast, saved the scan and sent it to Woody's drop box. He waited a few minutes before he signed on to Megaland.

Megaland: Welcome back, Picasso2B. Thought I'd lost you to soccer season or something.

Picasso2B: Yeah right. I'm hardly a soccer boy. Just drawing.

Megaland: Cool.

Picasso2B: Did one you'll like, based on a girl I know. Sent it to your drop box.

Inky kept his comments short. Now that he knew about Woody's past, he didn't much feel like chatting. But he had to be sure he didn't say anything wrong or make Woody suspicious.

Megaland: Lemme check.

He has to like it, Inky thought. The cursor blinked. Inky was nervous. This was how he was going to protect Amanda. What if Woody didn't want him to deliver the picture? What if his drawing wasn't good enough to make him interested?

Finally Woody returned to the chat box.

Megaland: It's a little blurry. Do you have more?

Inky didn't believe that he could have messed up the scan. He checked the scanner settings, checked for any smudges on the glass and reopened the file. There was no way the image he sent was blurry.

Picasso2B: Must be the drop box. Let me resend.

Megaland: Try a different section.

Yes, Inky thought, it's working. He wants to see more. Woody wanted his drawing. Well, he'd make him want it even more. He selected a section of the drawing that showed more of the breast, scanned it, sent it and waited.

Picasso2B: Sent

It took several minutes for Woody to return to the chat.

Megaland: Oh this is good. You are a *.

Inky could picture Woody salivating.

Picasso2B: Tnx. glad that u appreciate my work. It's not something I can show to just anyone.

Megaland: I'd love to see the whole thing

Picasso2B: too big to scan

Megaland: You could keep doing it in sections.

Picasso2B: That's a lot of work. It's really big.

Megaland: I could send a messenger. Leave it with your doorman.

Picasso2B: No doorman

Megaland: How about your super?

Picasso2B: Absentee landlord.

Megaland: Bummer.

Inky hoped he hadn't presented so many obstacles that Woody would lose interest.

Picasso2B: So, my school project really worked out well. You helped me out, really encouraged me. I'd like to do something for you in return. I can drop this drawing off for you.

Megaland: That's a kind offer.

"Michael, telephone. One of your classmates," Inky heard his mother yell out. Who was calling on the landline? He couldn't think of a worse time, and if it was one of his old Culture Club friends, now was not the time to rekindle a friendship.

"Just a second, Ma," he called out. He could feel his heart racing. If he told her to take a message, he'd have to talk to her. He knew he had to show her his project, and that would be intense. First he had to protect Amanda.

Picasso2B: GTG. POS. Shoot me yr address. I'll drop it off after school or the weekend or something.

The cursor blinked.

"Michael," his mother called.

"Coming, coming," he said. But there was no way he was leaving the computer until he saw that address. Not that he actually needed it. Thanks to Rungs, they had that and more. What he did need was for Woody to offer it, to agree to have Inky deliver the picture to his studio.

Picasso2B: Really gtg. Where should I drop this off?

Megaland: The studio's in an iffy neighborhood.

Picasso2B: I'm a New Yorker – everything's gentrified

Megaland: LOL

Inky hoped that meant Woody was going to give him his address. But the cursor blinked and the textbox was unchanged. What was taking him so long? And who was still holding on the landline? Inky realized he hadn't given Amanda his cell phone number and the landline was the number listed in the school directory. It had to be her, and he hated to keep her waiting. What was Woody doing? Was he changing his mind?

Then the chat box opened and Inky saw Woody's address. It matched what Rungs had come up with. He pumped his fist in the air. The plan might work after all.

Picasso2B: No problem, I can get there. Saturday, then.

Inky signed off quickly, before Woody had a chance to object. He ran to the phone in his room and heard Amanda's voice. He was grateful that at least his mother hadn't yelled out, "It's a girl." He didn't want Amanda to know what an infrequent occurrence that was. Actually, no one called anymore.

Inky apologized breathlessly.

"What took you so long? Were you drawing?" she asked.

"Sorry."

"I talked to Hawk," she said. Amanda's voice was soft and bright, a spring green. It was almost better to talk to her on the phone and imagine her face. Except that Inky had never really been good on the phone. He got caught up in the images in his head and tended to nod rather than speak.

"Are you there?" she asked.

"Yeah, sorry. Hawk . . ."

"I didn't have to go far to find her. She was skateboarding in the plaza outside my building."

Inky laughed. "So, Hawk."

"So we can use her driver. We just have to drop her at the hospital."

"The hospital? Why the hospital?"

"Hawk volunteers at the hospital every Saturday—with kids with parents with cancer."

Another heavy conversation in my future, Inky thought. "That's pretty dope."

"What?"

Inky thought it was cute that Amanda didn't get slang. "It's great that she does that."

"Yeah. Said she couldn't let them down when they need someone to talk to."

Inky winced. Hawk was doing for others what he'd been unable to do for her.

"I could tell she wanted to come with us," Amanda said.

"It's great that you convinced her." Inky was relieved that Hawk hadn't insisted on coming along. "Are you nervous?"

"Yes. No. You and Rungs have this figured out."

Sure hope so. "Tomorrow Rungs and I are posing as tourists to check out Woody's street. You were right to call him Spyboy, Amanda." He liked saying her name.

"He's a natural at all this."

"It's in his blood." Inky changed the subject from Rungs. "You know, if you don't want to do this, all you have to do is say so."

"I'm in," Amanda said. "Like I told Hawk, this is being brave for all the right reasons. It's the most important thing I've ever done."

Chapter 34
Ready, Set, Go

INKY REMOVED HIS SHOES and Rungs shuttled him into a small room stacked with gadgets and gizmos, recording equipment and computers. Inky noted a small placard over the inside doorway in Rungs's handwriting that said "heaven."

The housekeeper insisted on bringing them snacks, and Inky found he couldn't stop eating the pink and white puffed salty crisps. He'd finished half the bowl by the time Amanda arrived.

She was dressed in the layers that Rungs had suggested—a tank top under a peach cardigan. Her hair was loose. A strand of her bangs fell into her eyes.

"I need that hair clip," Amanda said.

Inky picked up her butterfly clip on top of a blinking machine. She brushed the stray bangs away from her eyes. They were close, almost close enough to kiss. It made his hand shake, so it looked like the butterfly in his hand was moving. He pretended the butterfly was flitting towards Amanda and put it in her hair. She laughed.

She touched the clip. "Wow, this feels ordinary to me," Amanda said, turning the clip over. Inky looked over her shoulder.

"It is," said Rungs.

"Whatd'ya mean? There is a hidden microphone, isn't there?" asked Amanda. Inky heard a bit of panic in her voice.

"Couldn't do it. Too much risk of it being found."

"There's no microphone?" Amanda's voice was a mix of worry and anger.

"But, but . . ." Inky started.

"There would have to be a wire from the clip through Amanda's hair and down her back," Rungs said. "You need a transmitter on site, meaning on her body, to send the signal so we can hear and record what is going on. Think of what could happen if he found it."

Color drained from Amanda's face, and she shot a pleading glance at Inky. Inky was still stuck on the "if he found it" part.

"Also, if he had her putting on any kind of costume or props—like a cheerleader's skirt or some slinky outfit, the fabric could've done the mic in. Total fail."

"Dude, we have to hear what's going on," he said to Rungs. "What if he tries something?"

"Don't say that," Amanda said sharply, walking over to the window to glance at the gray late-fall sky outside.

"We do have to be able to hear what's going on, and you said we have to make a tape," Inky said.

Rungs held up an ordinary looking cell phone. "Check this out."

"What's so great about that? It doesn't even look like a new smartphone." Inky said, rolling his eyes in Amanda's direction. She chewed on the side of her lip. "If we can't hear what's going on, we don't have a leg to stand on," Inky said.

"What? Where are you standing?" Amanda asked.

When this is over, I'm going to have to school her in American English, Inky thought. "Rungs was just getting around to telling us," he said.

"Check it," Rungs said, undaunted by Inky's cut. He handed Amanda the phone that looked like the standard issue freebie. "I found this baby in my dad's bag of tricks."

Amanda looked at him skeptically and did not take the phone from him. "Thanks, but I brought mine. It's the newest iPhone."

"So you think this is just some phone? It can dial out and receive calls like any other mobile phone," Rungs said. "And to look at it, you wouldn't think it could do much more."

"Got that right," Inky said.

Amanda looked at Rungs hopefully.

"This phone is actually a powerful personal detective tool. An infinity transmitter. It has built-in super sensitive microphones. You can hear any sound in the vicinity of the phone once you activate the special program. There's no range limit, and no danger of being discovered, like with wires on your body.

"How do you turn on the program?" Inky asked.

"Just a couple of text messages. There's no change on the display, nothing to indicate that it's transmitting what's going on. And from the receiver in the car, we'll be able to hear it all clearly and tape it to use as evidence."

Amanda held her hand out for the phone, which Rungs passed to her. "Feel better?" he asked. She smiled and nodded yes.

"You do need to have your bag as close as possible to you at all times," Rungs said.

"It's cool for you to use it?" Inky asked.

"Consider it field testing. One of my chores—all my dad's equipment has to be checked once a month anyway. They don't want to have an agent in the field with a device filled with dust kittens."

Inky looked over to Amanda. "I know, they're not real cats," she said.

They heard a ring from Amanda's purse. Inky looked over at Rungs, thinking this was more of his preparation. Amanda must have thought that, too. She picked up the spy phone. Nothing happened.

"Hey," she said. The phone continued to ring.

"Hey, what," Rungs said. "Answer your iPhone."

Amanda stuck her tongue out at him as she picked up her phone.

"It's Hawk," Amanda said. "I'll go meet her downstairs."

* * *

"You're flying solo?" Hawk said, getting out of the long black sedan. Amanda bristled at her tone of voice.

"Inky and Rungs are packing up the recorder and receiver. They'll be down in a second," Amanda said. She put her index finger in her mouth and chewed on a hangnail.

"Nervous, huh?"

"I'm OK." She looked at the purple strand of hair hanging below her chin and wrapped it around her finger.

Hawk pointed at her finger. "Don't cut off your circulation."

"You're not helping. Why are you doing this?" Amanda said.

"I am helping," Hawk said, "if I may remind you. Who arranged the car and driver for you?"

Amanda felt the color drain from her face. She didn't want to say anything that could jeopardize their arrangements. She tried to push back the anger she was feeling. Was Hawk trying to get her to back out or something? Amanda smiled as sweetly as her rising anger would allow.

"I'm just helping 'cause I figure I owe you—I never thought you'd say that shit. It was *epic*. No one feels sorry for Ellen, you know."

Amanda found this news comforting. Maybe she wasn't going to be such a pariah after all.

"But why are you doing *this*?" Hawk asked. "Inky needs all the friends he can get. You don't have to do something crazy for him."

Amanda glared at Hawk.

"Well? You're the one who could get hurt."

"Oh, Hawk. Don't scare me any more than I'm already scared, OK?" Amanda touched Hawk's shoulder. "Remember when you asked me if I'd ever done anything brave? Well, this is it. I know I'm taking a big risk, but I'm doing something that matters. I'm being brave because some other girl may not be."

Amanda turned around to see Inky and Rungs coming out of the building. "And because I have friends who help me be brave," she added.

Hawk fumbled with the buttons of her burlap "Feed" bag, then pulled out her phone. For a second Amanda was afraid she'd call the driver or her father or someone and call it all off because she mouthed off.

"You included," she said to Hawk.

"Take my phone. My dad's name and bank show up on caller ID. You won't believe the response 'World One Bank, President' will get if you have to call the police or something."

How ironic, Amanda thought. Two weeks ago I had no phone at all. Now I have three.

"Trade," Amanda said, handing Hawk her phone. The only people she wanted to talk to were already with her.

* * *

The four of them were squeezed together in the back of the car, their individual space even more limited because the receiver hung over Rungs's lap and took up room on the seat. He fiddled with the settings.

"Yeah, baby, WTG," Rungs said softly, looking with satisfaction at the blue light on the receiver. "Way to go." He patted the top of the machine.

Hawk glanced over at the equipment, and Inky saw her longing. She wanted to be part of this, but she wasn't going to bail on her group of kids in need. Respect, he thought as he met her gaze and quickly looked away.

It was uncomfortably silent in the back of the car. Inky stared at the broad shoulders of the driver through the plexiglass divider, his thick neck and shaven head suggesting power. He took advantage of the tight seating and leaned into Amanda on his left and pointed to Central Park in front of them as they drove crosstown.

"Wouldn't have thought you had this in you," Hawk said to Inky. He was grateful for the break in the silence. He took her words as an apology.

"Things are not always what they seem—that's for sure. People do what they have to do," Inky said, forging a truce.

Hawk nodded and smiled. "I hear you, Artboy."

"Here you go, Miss Helen," the driver said, pulling up to a building next to Roosevelt Hospital. Suddenly Inky was tense. How much time would they have? How long could her session be? But apparently Hawk had already thought of this.

"I'm going to do some shopping and stuff after, Ivan," Hawk said to the driver. "Please stay with my friends."

Rungs looked up from his receiver. "Thanks, Hawk."

She hugged Amanda, and said, "Good luck. And call me." Inky thought he saw Amanda giggle, which puzzled him. Hawk got out of the car and started to walk away. Then she turned and tapped on the driver's window. He lowered it, letting in a cold blast of air. "Whatever they need, Ivan, no matter what."

* * *

As they drove toward Megaland Studios, Amanda spread out a bit but shivered into Inky.

Inky watched the Hell's Kitchen streets through the partially opened window. "We're just about there," he said. Amanda took Rungs's phone out of her purse and checked the time. Inky looked at the display. Ten minutes until she was due at Woody's, and they were just a couple of blocks away.

"Let's test the phone again," Inky said to Rungs.

"You're going to keep that near you at all times," Inky said. He thought that Amanda could hear the worry in his voice.

Rungs sent a text message to the phone in Amanda's hand. Inky looked at a string of gibberish on the tiny display.

"Hit OK," Rungs said to Amanda.

Amanda complied. Inky looked at her wrist, the lovely curve between her forearm and hand, and the spot where the little round bone protruded and made an elegant slope. His fingers itched for a pencil. He shook his head to keep his focus. He would remember this. He touched her lightly on the arm. She didn't pull away.

"Now don't do anything," Rungs said. Inky felt his cheeks burn even though the words were meant for Amanda. He thought his friend could tell he had other things on his mind. He looked at the phone in Amanda's hand. For a barely discernible second the lights behind the phone's keypad illuminated, then went off.

"OK, you're set," Rungs said.

Then Amanda handed Hawk's phone to Rungs. "Use this when you call the police," she said. Inky looked at her, then over to Rungs. "Hawk's . . ."

"Brilliant," Rungs said. "Her father's caller ID." Inky could see Rungs refining their plan to include this.

"Don't accept any food or anything to drink," Rungs said to Amanda. His voice was picked up by the phone in Amanda's hand and fed back through the receiver. First there was a high-pitched sound, then Rungs twisted a knob and the screech stopped. Rungs's voice was doubled, with a slight delay, giving it an impactful echo.

"Nothing. He may try to drug you."

Inky shuddered at Rungs's words. He sensed that Amanda did, too. "You can still back out," Inky said to Amanda.

"Don't tempt me," she said.

Chapter 35
So This Is It

THE CAR TURNED DOWN WOODY'S STREET. On the left was a low row of brick buildings. There was a rusted sign for AAAuto. Another shop offered floor tiles. Above it, a woman in a floral dress was shaking out a rug from a fire escape. Inky spotted what looked to be a factory building next to a building with boarded-up bay windows. There was no sign, but there was a flagpole holder where the Megaland Studios banner they'd seen in the online pictures must have hung. It looked dumpier than the old promo pictures they'd found online.

"This is where we want to go, but could you go around the block and park by the car repair place?" Rungs said to the driver.

The driver circled the block. This was the block that Inky would walk down later to deliver the artwork to Woody, setting the end of the plan in motion. The thought was like a puddle of colors swirling together on a palette, muddy and confused. If he felt this way, what must Amanda be feeling? Inky took Amanda's hand and squeezed it as the driver idled the car.

Rungs gave his final set of instructions. "Remember everything we went over. Don't let him back you into a corner. Know where the door is. If you say 'emergency' your phone is programmed to dial the police. We'll hear everything that's going on. It'll be like we're there with you."

"You're about as comforting as soap in a rainstorm," Inky said. He wanted the floorboards to swallow him up. Why did he say something so stupid?

Amanda looked at him, shook her head and giggled in spite of herself. "Soap in a . . . that's just strange."

"I know, right. But I got you to smile," Inky said, leaning closer to Amanda. Her skin was a vanilla crème color, so inviting. Inky touched her cheek. He leaned in towards her and could feel her closeness. Her lips were a perfect strawberry red, with a little spot in the corner slightly swollen where she'd been biting it.

"Be sure to speak up," Rungs said. "Let him think you're a loud talker. We want to be sure to hear you."

Inky was still precariously close to Amanda. He should let her listen to Rungs's advice, he knew, but he couldn't move away. And she wasn't pulling away either. She was looking at him so intently he felt like she was drawing him closer with her eyes, as if there were a magnet in them.

Be brave, Inky told himself. That's what today's all about. He leaned in some more and kissed

Amanda on the lips. It was more than a quick peck. His lips lingered before they opened slightly and he pulled his head back.

He saw a look of surprise in her eyes. It must have mirrored his own. He'd just kissed Amanda. Kissed Amanda, here in the car, in front of Rungs. Ugh. His friend would have something to say about that.

He'd thought so much about this day, going over every possible detail in his mind, night after sleepless night. But he hadn't imagined that this would be the day he'd kiss Amanda. He hadn't allowed himself to think that he'd kiss her at all. A sea of neon colors swirled in his head. He could still feel the warmth of her lips on his. Amanda smiled a smile that said she was surprised, in a good way.

"Ahem. Ahem," Rungs said. "Hate to interrupt, but it's time."

Inky felt the blood rush to his cheeks, but he didn't really mind the embarrassment. He had kissed Amanda. His legs felt jumpy, like he'd eaten too much sugar.

"You OK?" Inky asked Amanda.

She nodded. "You?"

He squeezed her hand as an answer. He wanted to hold on to it. He wanted to say, "Don't go."

She looked over at Rungs as she opened the car door. "We've got your back," he said.

Inky watched her get out on the traffic side. "Careful, the traffic."

Amanda laughed. There were no cars coming down the street.

"We'll be listening," Inky said, "and I'll be there soon." Inky took a deep breath as the door closed. He wanted to run out and get her.

From the sidewalk Amanda turned and looked into the car. "Wave if you can hear me," she said. Rungs raised his hand. She made a thumbs-up gesture as she approached Megaland Studios.

Rungs adjusted the receiver between them on the car seat.

"So now will you admit that you *like* like her?" Rungs asked.

Inky nodded and broke into a huge grin. His face felt funny—he couldn't remember the last time he'd smiled that way.

Inky heard rustling coming from the speaker. It was no louder than the muted phone conversation the driver was having. Rungs turned up the volume and they heard the sounds of the street. Inky closed his eyes and was able to pick out the sound of Amanda's footsteps. The footsteps of the girl he'd kissed.

Say something, Inky thought. Describe what you're seeing. As if he'd willed it, he heard Amanda's voice.

"So this is it." Amanda was speaking softly in a voice that could be mistaken for her talking to herself. He heard the sound of the door opening, then the street noise was muted as it closed. "Megaland Studios."

Chapter 36
Justagirl in Megaland

AMANDA HIT THE BUZZER. "Who's there?" came right away, as if someone had been waiting by the buzzer expectantly. Even through the muffle of the intercom, Amanda could tell that Woody was smiling.

"It's me, Justagirl." It felt weird saying her screen name aloud.

"I'm coming right down."

Her stomach did a flip. The voice was raspy but melodic. She thought she heard the same local accent that one of the doormen in her building had. She wasn't sure what he'd look like based on hearing his voice. Inky was probably good at that. Inky, who she'd kissed in the car. The thought made her smile. Her first real kiss. Already it had been quite a day.

Amanda heard footsteps. For a moment she wanted to turn and run. "Oh god," she said. He was moving quickly down the stairs. Her heart raced. His steps seemed light. At least he's not fat, she thought, or he's an awfully quick fat man.

What was she going to say to him? They'd practiced a couple conversations to be sure she didn't give away any information about herself, or about Inky and Rungs. But knowing what she couldn't say wasn't the same as knowing what *to* say. And things didn't always go as planned.

Amanda tapped her purse as a reminder that Inky and Rungs were listening. The footsteps were louder, closer. Amanda looked out the glass building door, even though the car was parked out of view, halfway down the street.

She saw his tan Frye boots and acid washed jeans first. The jeans were carefully pressed, which somehow made her feel better. He was tall, slim, and as she looked up, she was surprised that he was handsome, in a weathered, fatherly kind of way, with long salt-and-pepper hair, very old school, but carefully trimmed. The wrinkles around his eyes made them seem happy, twinkling.

"Is it really you?" he said, smiling down at her. He opened the inner door wide and half bowed to her. "I told you you were beautiful.

"Come in, come in. I'm Woody," he said, sticking his hand out. *Bien élevé*, she thought. He has good manners.

"Glad to meet you," she said, echoing his politeness. She was glad that he didn't look like a monster. In fact, he didn't look dangerous at all. Maybe Inky and Rungs had been wrong. "I'm Justagirl—but my friends call me Amanda."

Woody gestured for Amanda to head up the stairs. She thought she felt him looking at her as she climbed. At the top of the stairs was a long carpeted hallway. The blue-flecked carpeting was frayed. She could smell cigarettes. Amanda looked at the gold records on the wall. She didn't recognize any of the songs or band names.

"Are these real gold?" she asked.

"They're real gold records. All these bands recorded here. Megaland was a happening studio back in the day." He winked at her. "The plaque is just a vinyl record dipped in metallic paint." He was charming, much in the way that Hawk exuded personal power, which both scared her and made her envious.

Woody opened the door to the studio lounge. Above the black leather couch were framed pictures of Woody looking hip and mugging it up with various skinny-legged guys with big hair and cigarettes hanging out of their mouths.

"Some set of pictures. A different world. Sometimes it feels like it was a different planet," Woody said. He hadn't stopped looking at her.

Amanda giggled. The pictures were funny, like caricatures almost. But the giggle continued for too long, riding on a wave of relief, and threatened to go out of control. Amanda pinched herself to stop.

"Let me show you the rest," Woody said, not commenting on her giddiness. He put his hand on her shoulder to lead her. It was a polite, chivalrous gesture. It gave her the creeps.

The main room was a huge space with some smaller rooms off of it, one of which appeared to be where he slept. "This was the control room. The board—all the faders and dials and knobs—used to be here. Now it's my work room," Woody said as he pointed to several computers lined up on a workstation. Amanda noticed a blue velvet curtain suspended in an area in the corner.

Woody pointed to the old overstuffed armchair across from the workstation. "Have a seat."

She tucked her purse at her side and shifted in the chair. Woody sat in one of those fancy computer chairs across from her. She felt like she was in her father's office.

"Can I get you something to drink? Lemonade? Hot cocoa?" He walked over to the kitchen area and held up the packet of cocoa. The packet shook. He was as nervous as she was, she thought. This mattered to him, too, but she didn't know if the reason should make her feel worried or flattered. Maybe he just liked her.

"How about some tea?" he asked, definitely trying to please her.

It would be the polite thing to do to say yes, but she remembered what Rungs had said.

"I'm not thirsty now. I had a big soda on the way, but maybe later."

"Here, pick some music," he said, pointing at a case of CDs next to her chair.

She leaned over and scanned the band names: Nirvana, Van Halen, Jimi Hendrix, Crack the Sky, aware all the while that he was looking at her. "I don't listen to any of these bands."

"Must seem like dinosaur music."

"I missed a lot of music—haven't really lived in the States."

Woody picked a U2 CD and popped it in the CD player and walked over to the velvet curtain. He reminded her of a lizard scurrying about. "At least I didn't show you my record collection. So, am I what you expected?"

Amanda didn't see that question coming, even though Rungs had warned her that Woody would make the conversation personal. She felt her cheeks flush. "I don't know. I just met you—well, not really. Kind of. You're, I don't know. Uh, cool." Was that the right thing to say? She was so uncertain, and knowing that Inky and Rungs were listening in just made her even more tongue-tied.

"I have a present for you," he said, reaching behind the velvet curtain.

"A present?"

Woody brought her a large rectangular box in silver and purple wrapping paper. It looked like it came from a fancy boutique.

"Pretty wrapping paper," Amanda said.

"Open it," Woody said as he darted back behind the curtain. Amanda stared at the box. She didn't want to open the present while he wasn't in the room.

"G'head. Open it," he said, popping out from the curtain with a professional-looking heavy black camera in his hands.

Amanda's hand shook as she tore the wrapping away. It was the thick kind, the kind her mother would keep in a box when they were in Nairobi to reuse for other gifts or for school projects.

"I'll take your picture while you open the box. Sometimes candids are fun, too," Woody said as a flash went off in Amanda's face.

* * *

Inside the car the sound of the paper rustling was so loud that it almost blew out Inky and Rungs's ears. Rungs turned down the volume. This is so creepy, Inky thought as they heard the sounds of ripping paper. He felt like he did when he was really young and listened to his parents' conversations through their closed bedroom door: embarrassed and confused. It made him sad to think of his parents together. Rungs's voice brought him back to the present.

"That's a box, a lid coming off a box," Rungs said, indentifying the popping sound they heard.

"Oh, my god," they heard Amanda exclaim. "Is it really? They're amazing."

"Tell us what it is," Rungs said.

The sound became muffled. "She must've put the wrapping paper and box on top of her purse. Hear how the levels changed?"

Inky nodded, but he was thinking about more than the tape sound. Whatever was in the box, he didn't want her to like it. He didn't want anything to tempt her to let her defenses down, and he didn't want her to feel too kindly toward Woody. After this was over, he'd have to think of a gift to give her that she'd really like.

"I can't believe it. They're the same, aren't they? They're the boots from Megaland. The high boots from the closet dress-up game?"

"Good girl," Rungs said. "Keep narrating. Tell us everything that's going on."

They heard footsteps coming towards Amanda.

"Try them on," they heard Woody say to Amanda.

"Creep," Inky said to the voice coming out of the receiver. "Stay away from her. Keep your freakin' distance."

"Quiet!" Rungs said.

They heard more rustling. Amanda's voice was harder to hear. "Size eight," she said.

"She must be bending over. See how her voice changed," Rungs said. Glad he's enjoying this, Inky thought, then felt badly for thinking that. Rungs was good at this, and if it weren't for him, they might never have come up with this plan to begin with.

"How'd you know?" Amanda asked Woody.

"That's the box you clicked on in the dress-up closet in the game. I guessed you might pick your real size."

"Whoa," Inky said. "Clever bastard."

They heard some shuffling and then Amanda's voice sounded farther away as she made appreciative noises about the boots. Then they heard the electronic sound of a camera.

"Yuck," Inky said. He looked down at his artwork, carefully rolled, sitting on the floor of the car. He wanted to deliver it now. He wanted all this to end.

"They're perfect. I love them," Amanda said.

"G'head. Walk around. Let me see for sure that they fit you—you know, like how you do it in the shoe store," they heard Woody say.

They heard footsteps, softer footsteps than before. Footsteps walking away from the microphone. Amanda's footsteps. Why'd she have to be so cooperative? Inky thought.

"Are you ready for some posed pictures? I have a lot of costumes and props." Woody's voice seemed louder.

"Sure," Amanda said, from what seemed to be more of a distance.

"C'mon, talk to us, tell us what you're doing," Rungs said.

Inky heard Amanda's soft footsteps. "Back here?" she said.

"Behind the curtain," Woody answered.

When Amanda spoke again, it sounded even more distant, her voice subdued, like how a color was diluted when he added water to an ink wash.

"Wow. You have some unusual clothes here," she said.

Inky opened the window, but the outside noises made it too hard to hear the transmission of what was going on in the studio. He closed the window again. The driver glanced back disinterestedly and turned back to the action scene on the DVD he was watching.

Inky heard a scraping sound and closed his eyes to try to get a picture. Hangers, it was the sound of hangers on a rack.

"This is better than my mother's closet 'cause they're all cute." Inky hated that Amanda sounded like she was having fun. He thought of how Woody had been so charming and so supportive, when all he really wanted was to use Inky's artwork to lure young girls. Yuck. Now he was being charming with Amanda. And she was up there alone.

Inky looked over at Rungs. "That's enough. I'm gonna ring the buzzer."

"Not yet," Rungs said. "We need him to take a couple of pictures."

"Shh!" Inky said. He had to hear what Amanda said next. He didn't want any of Rungs's reasoning.

"Ooh, a Halloween costume. Is this a maid's outfit?"

"I gotta go in there," Inky said.

Rungs pressed his arm against Inky and held him back. "Soon. Very Soon." Inky sat back halfway.

"Ooh, look at this." Amanda sounded like she was faking enthusiasm. Or maybe he just wanted to hear it that way. "I love the beads and the V neck."

"Hold it up against you," Woody said to Amanda. His voice sounded more muffled. He must be standing closer to Amanda, Inky thought.

Inky pushed Rungs's arm away and reached down for his artwork.

"That's lovely," Woody said. "It looks really sophisticated. It'll show off your long legs. Let me take a picture of you in it. Here, you can change behind this curtain. The catch can be tricky. I'll help you with it."

Chapter 37
Picasso2B in Megaland

INKY'S HAND WAS ON THE CAR DOOR handle. He pressed down halfway and it clicked. The driver looked up from the DVD player on the front seat, turned his head halfway, gave Inky a disinterested glance and turned back to his DVD.

Rungs stretched out his arm and held Inky back. "Let's call it in first," he said as he picked up Hawk's cell phone and dialed.

"I'm counting on caller ID here," Rungs said, and dialed the Midtown North precinct, a couple of blocks away.

Counting on Hawk was more like it. But Inky knew this time she'd come through. While her mother was so sick, her father still traveled a lot. It fell to Hawk to supervise her mother's care, and that, he knew, had included several emergencies.

"An officer is needed, six hundred block of West 53. Request arrival without lights or sirens," Rungs said in a put-on adult voice that almost convinced

Inky. Rungs was also mimicking the trace of a German accent that Hawk's father had.

Rungs gave Inky a thumbs-up. Inky assumed the officer on the other end had asked about the nature of the crime.

"Level 2 sex offender, William Turner, ID number 28292, in violation of parole; violation of the no-contact with minors clause, possible intent to engage in questionable activity with a minor. Request caution, minor present," Rungs said, the fake accent less pronounced.

Just as Rungs finished with the police, Amanda's voice came through the receiver. "I can do this myself," she said. Her voice sounded wobbly.

"Let me make it easier," Woody responded.

"Really, I'm good," she said. It sounded like she was stepping away from him.

"I don't want to leave her up there any longer," Inky said to Rungs.

"Precinct house is a few blocks away," Rungs said. "They'll be here any second."

They heard Amanda's footsteps, the soles of her new boots tapping on the wood floor, then Woody saying, "You look lovely."

A second later they heard the mechanical whir of a digital camera. "Hold that," Woody said to Amanda.

Inky clutched his drawing and opened the car door. "That's it. I'm outta here. It'll take him some time to get downstairs," he said to Rungs as he got out of the car. "The police'll be here by then."

Inky didn't wait for Rungs's reaction. He walked by the auto repair shop. His swift steps were so strong he could feel the sidewalk through his sneakers. He passed the boarded-up building and noticed a lady cleaning furniture on a fire escape. The studio was a few buildings away. Was Woody still taking pictures of Amanda? What was he asking her to do? Inky shuddered at the possibilities and broke into a trot. He had to get there as soon as possible. He had to get to Amanda.

Then everything went dark.

There was something around his head. It was heavy and odorous. A chemical smell filled his nose. It combined with his panic to make him light-headed. He tried not to breathe.

He wanted to scream. He was afraid to scream. Would screaming blow all that they'd planned for? Would it mean danger for Amanda? He was braced for an attack, but he didn't sense anyone near him. Who wanted him not to see?

He had to see. Seeing was everything. "No, damn it. No," he screamed.

Inky sucked in a breath of the chemical, and the colors in his head went hazy. He thought of the art room at the school. The scent was familiar—turpentine!

He reached up to his eyes and felt a nubby, rough fabric on his face. He found the frayed end of the fabric and lifted it away. He gasped and took in the cold, fresh air.

"Lo siento mucho, lo siento," he heard a woman's voice say. It came from above him. The fire escape. The lady in the flowered dress on the fire escape cleaning her furniture. No one was out to get him, she'd just dropped her cleaning rag.

Like a painting by Utrillo, the once seedy street scene now seemed a thing of beauty. The rusty sign, the steel gray sky, the overflowing trash, all glorious in their contrast of color and light. The flowers on the dress that apologetic Hispanic woman wore now transformed into a garden path leading him straight to Amanda.

Inky looked down the street to the car. Had Rungs seen any of this? Probably not. He was busy waiting for the police.

Finally he was at the front of the studio. He texted Rungs that he was about to go in but got no response. He yanked at the big glass front door to the studio building and entered. He looked at the buzzer that said "Turner and Megaland Studios." What had Amanda been thinking when she faced this buzzer? What she was thinking now?

Inky noted that the door opened out. That would make it easier for him to step outside once Woody came down, so he could block Woody's view of the approaching police, and maybe keep him from running away. He wished he had timed how long it took for Woody to come downstairs after Amanda had rung the buzzer, but he'd been too busy straining to hear the sounds from the receiver. Probably it would take longer now. He was interrupting, after all.

Inky pushed in the black button. The sound of the buzzer went through him. What if Woody ignored it? Last night on the phone he and Rungs had decided if that happened, Inky would keep pressing the buzzer and talk to Woody through the intercom. They figured Woody would not want a scene with Amanda there. The doorway now seemed eerily quiet as he waited for Woody to acknowledge the buzzer.

Inky made a note of his distance from the door, how his back was to the wall and where he needed to stand to reach the door to open it. He stepped in and out, counting his steps. He felt like he was in the awful folk dance unit of gym class. He always came in at the wrong part of the music, and now he was afraid he'd mess this up, too.

He wished he could talk to Rungs, wished he knew what was going on with Amanda. They should have a two-way system the next time they did this, he thought, then caught himself. There would be no next time. It was hard enough to believe there was a *this* time.

* * *

Down the street, Rungs greeted the policemen. He was surprised to see two officers in the squad car; his father worked alone. He wondered what else he hadn't calculated. He had a vaguely metallic taste in his mouth as the police officer rolled open his window.

"I called." Rungs said, standing up as straight as he could, glad for his height but knowing there was no way he looked like the president of an international bank, which is what he knew they'd presume because he'd used Hawk's phone with her father's caller ID.

"This some kind of prank? 'Cause we have zero tolerance for that kind of thing."

"No, sir. Deadly serious," Rungs said. How to explain? He started walking toward the sedan that was serving as their command central. One officer followed. His name tag said "Hogan." His partner remained in the squad car.

Rungs started with the facts. "William Turner, offender 28292, was posing as a game developer. He made arrangements to meet my friend. She's inside now, Officer Hogan."

"Her phone?" the officer asked.

Rungs didn't confirm the officer's assumption. "I gather I don't have to tell you who Helen Stegmann is. How her father would do anything for her. Her father the bank pres—"

"Yeah, kid. We got all that . . ." Officer Hogan said.

Rungs was glad he didn't have to totally lie. He glanced down the street toward the studio. Good.

Inky hadn't stepped outside yet. He walked up to the car, thinking he might have won the policeman over. Officer Hogan, a few steps behind him, approached the driver's window.

"He's not part of this," Rungs said, and he opened the back door of the car. Hawk's driver looked back, alarmed. "It's OK, we called him," Rungs said to the driver loudly enough so he could hear through the plexiglass barrier. "It's about our friend upstairs."

Rungs heard Woody's voice coming from the receiver, then the whir of the camera. "She's with him now. He's taking pictures of her," Rungs said to Officer Hogan. The officer let out a low whistle.

"Got a diddler," he radioed to his partner.

Then they heard Inky's distorted voice; it was what Woody and Amanda were hearing from the intercom. Rungs smiled. Inky was saying exactly what they'd arranged. "It's me. Picasso2B, the kid who draws for Megaland. I have that new drawing you asked me to drop off." They'd thought that Woody wouldn't be able to ignore the request, not in front of Amanda, who was supposedly testing the site, and especially if Inky made it a point to say he was a kid.

Sure enough Rungs heard Woody say to Amanda, "Why don't you look through the makeup over there while I get the buzzer."

"Cool," Amanda said. "My mother doesn't let me wear makeup."

Officer Hogan looked at the receiver, then at Rungs. Rungs noticed a flush of anger at the top of his pudgy cheeks.

"It's connected to a G-phone," Rungs said. "She has it in her purse. The box has a speaker and an HD recorder." Rungs couldn't help bragging about the gear, but the look on the officer's face suggested he was less than thrilled seeing Rungs's fieldwork in action.

"Unauthorized civilian use—and a kid. What all are you trying to do? What are you trying to pull? I should confiscate that," the officer said.

"I wouldn't be doing that," Rungs said, stepping closer to the officer so he was uncomfortably close to his face. "It's property of the Sahmnakkhaogrong-hangshaat."

"The what?"

Rungs reached into his pocket for his father's business card and handed it to Officer Hogan. "Thai National Intelligence Agency." Rungs pointed to the lettering.

The officer studied the card. "You print this out on your computer?"

"No, sir."

The officer ran his fingers over the raised letters of the card. Rungs pointed to the equipment again.

"My father's."

What the hell?" He let out a whistle. "Tell you what though, son, in this country, what you got from this box, it's not admissible."

Rungs replied quickly, thinking Woody would soon be in the building entranceway with Inky. "Get his camera, then. She's 14. That should be all the evidence you need—that and the captures of their chats you can get from his computer." Rungs could see the officer was now interested.

The policeman whistled again. "Sarge is gonna love this if we bring it in clean."

Rungs looked down at his phone and saw the text message from Inky. "My friend just buzzed up. He's gonna make the guy come down to collect this drawing he really wants. It's his artwork the creep has been using to woo her."

"Grooming," Officer Hogan said, as if he was talking to a colleague. "They all do that shit."

* * *

Inky was sweating even though it was chilly in the doorway. He was growing impatient. He hit the buzzer again, this time sounding out two staccato bursts.

"Coming, coming," a voice came through the intercom a moment later. Inky jumped at the sound and knocked the drawing against the wall, bending an edge. Hearing Woody's voice made it all real, and that was scary.

Please don't do anything to Amanda, Inky thought as he strained to hear footsteps. He thought of his abandoned religious school education. He needed a real prayer now, but none came to mind. So he squeezed his eyes shut and said his father's name over and over again, hoping it would do.

Inky steeled himself and glanced out the door. Rungs was still out of sight, but hopefully with the police. But what if the police didn't believe Rungs? And what if Woody figured out they were trying to trap him?

It felt like forever to Inky, standing there, straining to hear Woody's footsteps. His mind saw only the neutral palate of the doorway. He memorized every detail. He could draw this scene over and over; he would always know just the way the light came in through the doorway, the same way he'd always remember the image of the charred remains from his father's plane crash.

And then he saw Woody.

He looked like the pictures they'd seen online, but it was still a shock to see him in person. He'd spent so much energy thinking about how creepy Woody really was that he was unsettled to find that he was just a regular guy, a trim and confident regular guy with a friendly smile.

"Hi there, Picasso in training," Woody said breathlessly. "I wasn't expecting you now. Sorry I can't invite you up. Big session. I just have a minute. But it's great to meet you. Great to meet you." He held out his hand.

Inky shifted his drawing to the other hand and shook Woody's hand. He wondered if Woody noticed how sweaty his palms were. Would he think anything of it, or just think that Inky was nerdy and graceless?

"So you're the guy behind Megaland. It's so exciting to meet you," Inky said, hoping he sounded sincere. "Er, thanks for saying all those nice things about my work."

"You're a real talent," Woody said in a manner that made Inky think of the way agents or advertising guys were portrayed in movies.

Inky tapped on the rolled-up drawing. "Let me show you this one." It wobbled in his hand and he hoped that Woody didn't notice the shake.

This next part would be the hardest of all: getting Woody to step outside. They wanted Woody out of the building so it would be that much harder for him to go back and destroy any evidence on his computer. Inky tried to sound unrehearsed. He looked around the little space they stood in and said, "It's really dark in here."

Inky leaned against the glass door, then released it just like he'd practiced while he was waiting for Woody to respond. It was an awkward gesture and he hoped that Woody would not be suspicious. Inky's foot and the hand with the drawing were outside the doorway.

Woody gave him a curious look. Inky stepped all the way out, taking two steps back. He awkwardly held the door for Woody to follow, thankful for his long arms, worrying that he'd lose his footing or that he'd trip and blow it all.

Inky waved the rolled-up drawing—his signal to Rungs. "I really like figurative art," he said, hoping to distract Woody. Woody nodded in response.

Inky had another maneuver; he had to position himself in such a way that Woody would not see Rungs and the police officer approaching. He did a bit of a pirouette; he stumbled, just enough so that Woody noticed.

"I'm nervous, I guess," Inky said. "I've never shown a piece like this before, and well, you know, you've been . . ."

Woody waved him off. "Of course, of course. I understand. All artists are vulnerable. This must be hard."

Inky felt soothed by Woody's response. He didn't seem that suspicious. As Inky rolled the rubber band off of his drawing, he was hit with a wave of guilt about what he was about to do. Megaland had been a good thing for him in a lot of ways.

The rubber band snapped and hurt his finger. "Damn," Inky said, and he felt tears well up in his eyes. He tried to fill his mind with a soft color, settled on the peach of the shirt that Amanda was wearing and recovered.

He opened the picture and held it up for Woody to see. As he raised it, he noticed a shift in the shadow down the street. It had to be Rungs. He held the picture up to Woody's eye level, so that it blocked his own face. He was afraid his expression of relief would betray him. It was so close to over, but so much could still go wrong.

His hands were shaking so much that Woody was having a hard time taking in the picture.

"Easy, easy. It's just art," Woody said. Inky knew he was looking at the contour of the girl's breast in his picture.

"You are a truly marvelous artist. So realistic," Woody said. He put a hand on the picture.

For a moment Inky forgot why he was there and let himself feel proud. "I'd love to show you more someday. I have a whole portfolio," Inky said, stalling. What was taking them so long? The car wasn't parked that far away.

"Let me just take this and I'll get back to you," Woody said. He seemed more hurried. Could he have caught a glimpse of the police car? "We'll make up a time when you can show me your whole portfolio. I know a lot of people." Woody started to reroll the poster in his hand and turned his body to go inside.

Inky's heart was beating so hard he felt like his chest could rip open. It was all so close. They'd worked so hard on all the details, but now Woody had the poster in his hand and he was turning to go upstairs. To go back to Amanda.

"Wait," Inky said too loudly. He could hear the panic in his own voice. Woody turned around.

"I really gotta run. Look I, er, it's my fault, Picasso, my friend. I shoulda had you confirm. I can't hold up a session—work being so scarce and all."

Woody's apology gave him a chance to compose himself. "I just wanted to sign it for you. I should have signed it. It was rude not to. Maybe, someday, you never know, maybe I will be a famous artist," Inky said, reaching into his pocket for a pen.

Woody sighed. "I have people waiting for me." He handed the poster to Inky.

Inky looked down the street and saw Rungs approaching. It was everything he could do not to smile in relief. "Yeah. I'll sign it and date it for you, too."

Inky shimmied over so that he was between Woody and the inner door. He held the picture up so that it was propped against the glass. His back was to Woody.

Inky could feel Woody watch him with impatient eyes as he put the pen to the poster and made the loop for a capital P and started to write "Picasso." Inky heard Rungs talking to the officers. Woody heard the voices, too. He whipped his head around to look down the street.

Inky glanced up at Woody's face and saw it turn white. He felt his heart pounding again. Had Woody seen the police with Rungs?

Woody shoved Inky hard to get him out of the way and grabbed at the door. Inky's shoulder blade hit the wall. The pain was a garish bright orange as it seared through Inky. He fell to the floor in a dizzy heap. It happened so fast. He'd dropped the poster and his fall had ripped it so that the head was now severed from the rest of the image. Amanda.

Woody fumbled with a key, which Inky assumed opened the inner door. Searing red flashed in his head. Woody was going to go back upstairs. Amanda was upstairs. Inky shot out his long leg in front of Woody, and made him trip.

The officers and Rungs entered the doorway.

Woody gave Inky a withering glance. "You?" he hissed.

Inky felt sick from the look of horror and betrayal on Woody's face. One of the officers reached out and grabbed Woody.

"William Turner," one of the officers said to Woody, "you are in violation of the terms of your parole as a Category 2 sex offender."

It seemed to Inky that Woody crumpled before him as he let out a low wail.

Rungs gave Inky a thumbs-up. He untangled his leg from in front of Woody and scuttled to his feet. One of the officers placed handcuffs on Woody. "You have the right to remain silent," he said.

As he continued, the other officer said to Inky and Rungs, "Let's go, boys. Let's tell your friend this is over."

Inky was already running up the stairs.

Chapter 38
Artboy and DiploKids
Bust Creep

A T THE TOP OF THE STAIRS, Inky was unsure which way to turn. He followed the wall of gold records, calling out Amanda's name. He entered a lobby area and yelled out, "Amanda, Amanda, it's over."

She ran to him and he opened his arms. As he drew her toward him, he could feel her shake.

"You are the bravest girl I've ever met," he said. He held her tight and rubbed her back, petting the soft peach sweater like a small animal. Gently, gently. A blossomy aura filled his head as she cried from relief, and he felt the warmth of her body against his. They said nothing but communicated everything while the officer, accompanied by Rungs, packed up Woody's computer and camera and gathered other evidence. Inky was unsure how long they stayed that way, but he knew it was long enough for him to feel the imprint of her on his chest; it felt like tomorrow had already come.

* * *

The hug was branded into his memory, white-hot and beautiful. It was that hug he thought of as he looked down at the beige stippled floor of the interview room in the police station while Rungs talked tech with Officer Hogan. The brown specks in the imitation stone pattern had too much red, but not enough to distract from the layer of dirt on the station floor. Inky would have liked to be near real rocks; actually, he would have liked to be any-where but there in the Midtown North precinct.

Mostly he wanted to be with Amanda, wanted to sit quietly with her and hear how she had felt each and every moment of that eventful day. He wanted to tell her again how proud he was of her, wanted to tell her about the moment when Woody looked at him, aware that Inky and his friends had busted him. She'd understand the muddy mix of pride and guilt he'd felt. He wanted to tell her how worried about her he'd been, wanted to hold her and tell her everything would be different now.

But that would have to wait while Officer Hogan and his partner debriefed them in that charmless room in the Midtown North precinct. Rungs, how-ever, was in his element, his natural habitat, as Mr. Wallingford, their science teacher, would call it.

Inky looked closely at Rungs, who had removed his sunglasses to talk to the officer. He could see the deep bags under his friend's eyes, as much of a badge of achievement as the one on the officer's uniform. Now Rungs reveled in the retelling of his nighttime code-cracking. He was drinking coffee with the cops, his jetlagged father alternately yawning and beaming at his son's accomplishments.

Rungs had been the first to comply with the police request for them to call their parents. He had reached his father, who was on the way home from the airport. Mr. R. had the cab take him directly to the police station, apologizing when he arrived for "not being fresh" after 24 hours of travel from Thailand.

The officers were deferential to Mr. Rungsiyaphoratana. "Just get it right," Inky had heard one of the bosses instruct the officers on the case. "Put on those kid gloves and don't make an international incident."

Amanda was hesitant to call her parents. "I'll get a historic talking-to," she'd said, with talking-to in air quotes as she illustrated the way her father got when he was mad. She puffed up her cheeks and made a face so grotesque she convinced Mr. R. to speak to her father first.

In the language known only to diplomats, Rungs's dad explained to Amanda's parents what had happened and smoothed it over for Amanda, so that instead of the scolding she expected, when she said, "Daddy, I'll tell you all about it, but now I just want to come home," he quickly said they loved her and they'd pick her up.

It was her mother who came in to the station, all glamorous and dramatic. Inky could see how much Amanda resembled her. "Maybe your father was right," Amanda's mother said, grabbing Amanda by the arm. "We should have gotten you a dog. You miss your brothers so. But Amanda, dear, how could you have made friends with this unsavory character?"

Amanda looked at Inky, then back at her mother. "It's complicated."

"Have you thought about what could have happened? This was a very dangerous thing you did, young lady. Your father told me not to overreact, but don't give me your shy, quiet routine."

Inky could see Amanda blush, and she almost seemed to shrink under her mother's words. Then she straightened her shoulders and smiled at him.

"It's OK, mama. I mean, a dog would be cool and all, but I have real friends now."

So do I, Inky thought, and beamed at her.

Then Rungs started talking again about the equipment and tracing the IP address to the studio. He reminded Inky of one of those trick birthday candles you blow out and after a moment it starts up again.

Inky saw the second policeman enter the room. He'd been questioning Woody. "Fine bit of work from you kids, fine bit of work," he said. "We got us a collar. Smart thinking to wait for him to take those pictures." Rungs's father put his palms together and bowed his head slightly in respect for the work his son had done.

Even though it was a weekend, Inky's mother was at work when he called. She was quiet while he explained about the game site and how Woody was so positive about his artwork, and how especially with everything going on with school and stuff at home, he'd been glad to have something that he wasn't failing at.

"I couldn't tell you about our plan. You would have been too afraid for me, too afraid to lose me. But the truth is, I was already lost."

"What would I do if something happened to you? What would I have done without you?" Inky's mother said.

Inky tried to tune out the officer who was tapping his foot impatiently while they spoke. "It worked out all right, Ma. But it's not like we've been so together." Inky disliked having this conversation on the phone in front of everyone. Thankfully Amanda and her mother were busy with paperwork and out of earshot.

His mother was quiet for a moment, and then said, "I know I haven't been there for you, Michael. It's just been so hard." Inky could hear her sob. "Your father, he was the expressive one. He was my balance. I don't know how . . ."

Inky hated it when his mother cried. She was always practical, stoic, the uber working mom.

"Mom, don't cry. It's OK. It's OK now. I mean, they're calling us heroes. Besides there's a reporter who wants to talk to us. Maybe you can tell us what to do."

Inky could feel her flex into her work mode, like the motor of his dad's old Saab when he shifted into the right gear and it started to run again.

"Here's what we'll do," she said. "After we sign whatever they need, why don't you invite your friends over and you can talk to the reporter then. We'll order in a feast for you and your friends, and their parents."

When all the paperwork was done and they were ready to go, Inky sought out Officer Hogan.

"Excuse me, officer. Could you tell me, did Woody say if there were other kids involved in this game?"

"Your guy was up to more than you knew about. Our search of his premises turned up evidence that his scheme with you kids was not his only endeavor. We're waiting for his lawyer to arrive so we can extract his confession."

"What else was he up to?" Inky asked.

"Afraid we can't tell you that just yet, but you've done a good thing."

* * *

Inky's mom had ordered a feast of Indian samosas and curries and had the big table set for eight.

Inky was amazed that she'd even remembered where the tablecloth was.

"It's been so long since we've had a gang of your friends over. Do you remember, Michael, how your father used to have everyone over? He used to say a bunch of you was easier than just one."

Inky looked around the table at his friends, then at the one empty seat, but before he could get sad about his father, his mother said, "I set a place for the reporter, too. Always a good idea to feed the press."

Rungs and his dad ate hastily and left before the reporter arrived. Mr. R. had suggested that Rungs not be present or named in the article due to the sensitivity of his job. Inky thought his friend would be more disappointed, but that was the thing about Rungs: you peeled back one layer and there was always something more, like those multi-colored grease pencils in the art room.

"It's about the doing," Rungs said. "Plus, I got my props from the cops. LYDK, that matters more to me than a thing in the paper. Like you didn't know."

"Besides," Rungs told Inky on the way out, "my dad's exhausted. And somewhere in his bag there's a letter and a tape from Apsara," Rungs said, referring to his girlfriend in Thailand.

"See ya later, Spyboy," said Amanda, who was there without her parents. Hawk laughed. Not the mean laugh that Inky had gotten used to hearing, but a soft, tinkling laugh. She'd come over with her dad. Mr. Stegmann was concerned about the possible mention of his bank. Inky's mother had handled that as soon as the reporter arrived and had started interviewing the adults.

"Don't put us in," Carol Kahn said to the reporter, someone she knew slightly from her corporate public relations work. "That the kids have prominent parents is not news. It's what they did, how clever they were, how brave. That's your story. And if you must say anything about their background, consider this: If these smart kids could get sucked in, anyone can. There's your story."

Then she led Mr. Stegmann to the living room. Inky heard the clink of wine glasses and Hawk's dad complimenting his mother on how she had everything under control.

Hawk played up her role, said she was the logistics coordinator or some such, but Inky didn't care. When Amanda retold her story, he got to look at her the whole time, noticing for the first time a freckle on her earlobe that looked like an earring. How could he have missed it? How much more was there to explore?

Amanda yawned and said she had to go. Her parents had asked her not to stay too long. Inky offered to walk her home.

Just outside his building, he saw the big tree he'd stare at from the window of his father's study. Most of the trees on the block were left barren from a midweek rainstorm, but this one held on steadfastly to a small crest of leaves. Inky pointed.

"It doesn't want winter to come yet," Amanda said, seeing what he saw. "But I don't mind."

Inky put his arm around her and steered her off the sidewalk and under the tree. He put two fingers on her face and turned her head towards his. She closed her eyes. He wanted his open, wanted to take in the softness of her skin, the length of her face, wanted to be sure he touched her lips with his. He watched her lip quiver, leaned in and let his lips meet hers, so soft and warm.

A leaf, the last vestige of fall, dropped from the tree and slowly fell, landing in her hair. She did not shake it out.

He was sure he said something to her and she said something back on the rest of the walk home, but all that Inky could think of was how unfamiliar his cheeks felt, uplifted in a smile.

* * *

It had been forever, or maybe never, that Inky was excited about going to school on a Monday. He dressed carefully, searching his drawer for his green striped shirt.

He was surprised that his mother had not yet left for work and was waiting for him at the breakfast table. She had gone for a run, showered and gotten bagels and a copy of the paper.

"Mom. Mom?"

"Thought you'd want to see this," she said, handing him the paper. "I don't always have to be the first one in the office."

He thumbed through the paper until he came upon the article with the headline "Artboy and DiploKids Bust Creep." He smiled at the use of Hawk's nickname for him. But even better, his sketch of the Green Goddess was used to illustrate the article. He thought how cool it would look in a frame hanging in his dad's study.

By lunchtime mostly everyone at MDA had seen the paper. Amanda and Hawk sat with Inky and Rungs at their usual table in the back. One by one their classmates made their way to the back to congratulate the group of them. Even Ellen Monahan. "Oh. My. God. You're amazing. Amazing. You all must sign the article," she said. While Hawk was signing the page, Ellen turned to Inky and asked, "Did you see his gold records?" Rungs sputtered coffee all over the paper, and Ellen left in a huff.

By last period assembly, all the attention was wearing thin. Inky wanted his friends to himself.

"I am so not ready to start another core project," Hawk said as they walked into the auditorium together. Inky and Rungs headed for their spot in the back, while Amanda and Hawk started down the aisle to some seats on the side. They laughed and froze in the aisle until one of the Soccer Boys they were blocking said, "You sitting, Artboy?" Some things never changed. They settled on four seats together in the middle.

Mr. Lorenza and Mrs. Patel told them about the next core project. This one would use their research, math and computer skills. It would be a study of the financial markets. Like the stock market challenge, but with a twist. Amanda frowned, but her expression changed when Mrs. Patel said they would be working in teams. Inky hoped his little group would get to work together.

Just when they thought there'd be early dismissal, Elsbet Harooni took the stage. Seeing the Principal still made Inky's stomach twist.

"Friends, I wanted to share the most exciting news," the Principal said.

"She got a new chair," Hawk whispered to Inky. He guessed Hawk had had her share of warnings, too.

"From time to time, you know, there are exhibits in the lobby of the UN. I've gotten word that next month's multi-panel display will be filled with the work of one of our MDA students. Now this space has often displayed the work of the IB project of our graduating students. At times, this honor has been shared by students in other grades in Upper School. It is my great pleasure to report that next month this display will be devoted to the work of an Upper One student. One of your core projects."

The room got quiet. Hawk had seemed about to make another Looney Harooni joke, but she, too, looked serious. Everyone had worked hard on their projects. A display at the UN, that was the kind of thing MDA parents—and students—loved.

"The multi-panel display, this month's exhibit, will feature 'Making Contact,' the presentation from Michael Kahn."

Inky gasped. Rungs clapped him on the back at the same time the students in the auditorium started clapping for him. The sensation was amazing. "Way to go, Artboy," someone shouted. Amanda kissed him on the cheek. Inky felt a rainbow of color, primary and pure.

He thought of an afternoon long ago looking with his father at the images in the giant lightboxes downstairs in Grand Central Station. He felt like he'd fulfilled a promise.

"Congratulations, Michael. Mrs. Patel will share the details with you in homeroom tomorrow. And for all of you, the financial markets project will start next week."

"Pinch me," Inky said to Rungs at their lockers. Hawk came by, with Amanda right behind her.

"We should celebrate," Amanda said.

"Later, definitely," Inky said. "Right now I have an appointment at Fresh Cuts. Gonna get this ponytail cut off and see if I can donate it to kid's cancer or something. Anyone wanna come?"

"I'm there," Amanda said.

"I'm out. Skateboarding with one of the kids from my talk group," Hawk said.

"Rungs?"

Rungs looked at Inky with a broad smile. "NCD. No can do. First day of my internship with the cybercrimes unit. But I'm gonna tell them all about you. They might need a good sketch artist."

AUTHOR'S NOTE

DRAWING AMANDA is a work of fiction, but the plight of indigenous people in Brazil and other nations is quite real. The Awa have been called the most threatened tribe, because of the encroachment of loggers and the destruction of rainforest lands. Survival International, one organization that advocates for the earth's threatened tribes, is a great resource for additional information.

ACKNOWLEDGMENTS

Thank you, Kenny, for your unfailing ear, support
and patience; Miles, for your good sense of my
story and yours, and thanks mom, for being a role
model for so much, especially discipline.

I'm lucky for the encouragement of friends - work
friends, mom friends, and amazing girlfriends. Writer
friends, including the mediabistro girls and Micol
Ostow, gave me valuable feedback along the way.

I'm eternally grateful to Rob Simon and the crew at
Hispo Media for plucking DRAWING AMANDA
from the submissions pile. Thank you for your hard
work and belief in me. And Sunny Lee, your
illustrations rock.

This book is for my father, who taught me to be
scrappy and persevere. I still miss him every day.

ABOUT THE AUTHOR

Stephanie Feuer's articles and essays have appeared
in *The New York Times, The Boston Herald,* on
bettyconfidential.com and in numerous anthologies
and literary magazines. She serves as creative
nonfiction editor of *Conclave, a Journal of Character.*
DRAWING AMANDA is her first published book of fiction.
She lives in New York City with her husband,
teenage son, Tibetan Terrier and an out of control
collection of books and CDs.
stephaniefeuer.tumblr.com or stephaniefeuer.com

ABOUT THE ILLUSTRATOR

S.Y. Lee received her BFA in Illustration from Syracuse University. Her work has been featured in children's books, textbooks, magazines, and on iPad® apps. She currently lives in New York with her two goldfish, One Fish and Two Fish. You can see more of her work on her online portfolio: callmelee.com

CPSIA information can be obtained at www.ICGtesting.com
Printed in the USA
BVOW01s2137170614

356670BV00001B/28/P